COLD BLOOD

COLD BLOOD

CALLIE HART™ BOOK TWO

RENÉE JAGGÉR

LMBPN PUBLISHING

LMBPN Publishing
PMB 196, 2540 South Maryland Pkwy
Las Vegas, NV 89109

First US edition, April 2020
Print ISBN: 978-1-64202-906-2

I sat on the passenger side of my car, fingers drawn into fists on my knees as I stared down the building. Inside, I'd find what I'd been hunting for a month. The truth that could change my life forever. Although Ronan and I had talked about the courts, I had not yet met a member of the summer court, and I wouldn't be making a decision until I did. However, I had located and ordered a critical piece of information that might help me make my mind up.

If only I could convince myself to go inside.

Come on, Callie, what are you afraid of? I blew out a long, deep breath. *You've been to war halfway across the globe. Just last month, you faced down a vampire assassin. Now you're shivering in your boots at the idea of picking up a paper?*

"Come on, Callie," my roommate, Sam, echoed. It was the Sunday of spring break at Ohio State, which meant sunbeams and sandy beaches in Spain as far as Sam was concerned. They just wanted me to get it over with, get a copy of my birth certificate, and get out so we could hit the road. There was a beach on Ibiza with our name on it.

I chewed my bottom lip and stared at the blocky building of brick and glass. Decorative iron spikes lined one section of the roof. I squinted up at them. "I don't know, Sam. Are you sure I should go in there? I mean, there's probably iron everywhere. I could get sick."

"That excuse didn't work when you had to go to the doctor last week for travel immunizations, and it's not going to work today," Sam informed me, crossing their arms over a t-shirt with a multicolored t-rex on it. In big block letters, the shirt read NON-BINOSAUR.

Sam was right. Ever since I'd found out I was half-fae, iron content was my favorite excuse. Didn't want to do the dishes? I'd try to get out of it by saying there was iron in the dishwasher. Take out the trash? No can do. Sam must've put something iron in there because my skin's getting all prickly. They were starting to get wise to it.

Sam nodded toward the front door. "You're going in there to get your birth certificate. Your *original* birth certificate, which has been locked away in a mysterious vault, just waiting for the day you came along. It's like a fairytale, Callie. Orphan girl with a rich benefactor finds out she was a princess all along."

I rolled my eyes at Sam. "This isn't a Disney movie. This is my life."

"Fae are real," Sam reminded me. "And magic, too. I'm just saying it wouldn't be totally unexpected if a pumpkin coach rolled up right now." They adjusted the rear-view mirror, just in case.

That was all I needed to convince me to get out of the car. If a pumpkin coach did show up, whatever stepped out of it probably wouldn't be friendly, and I didn't want to deal with any more monsters just now.

Sam hurried out of the car after me, but I didn't slow my walk to wait for them. If I did, I might stop and turn right back around. All week, I'd been trying to convince myself that I didn't need to know. Finding out whose name was on that birth certificate wasn't going to make my decision for me or reshape my future in any way.

In one week's time—right about when we got back from Spain—the winter queen would force me to choose a side. Fae weren't allowed to live without a court, not even half-fae like me. I didn't know what the consequences for not choosing were, but Mab had implied they wouldn't be pleasant. Too bad I hadn't been able to lay my hands on this one piece sooner.

At the very least, I'd lose my job as Ronan McCalister's bodyguard. Considering the very nice salary and the travel benefits, that wasn't something I wanted to happen. Never mind how much I actually enjoyed the job, even when Ronan was being weird, just as he had been leading up to this trip.

Inside, carpet muffled my footfalls as I walked up to the directory. The vital statistics office was down the hall. I frowned. There was a crowd in the waiting room nearby, but that was for the WIC office and the health department.

I'd been hoping for one last excuse to pop up so I could leave. A long line would've been perfect. I had to be at work in an hour, or else we'd miss our overnight flight to Barcelona. Ronan had two photoshoots out there as part of his modeling gig. Afterward, Ronan, Sam, and I had booked a weeklong vacation full of art galleries and beach-hopping. I was looking forward to the week off, even if it wasn't really a vacation per se. I'd still have to pull a few shifts guarding Ronan, but the new hires would fill in the gaps so we could always have two people on duty. No one was going to complain about a free trip to Spain. And I'd have time to read more of Walter's book. I hadn't managed to squeeze in a training course yet, but I had hopes for after we got back now that we had more people on board.

We went down the hall to a tiny window that the rest of the building almost seemed to have forgotten. A bored-looking middle-aged woman with glasses and plastic nails was at the window, but she ignored us in favor of whatever conversation she was having on the phone. I waited for a long minute.

Sam cleared their throat.

I gestured to the lady with my head as if to say, "She's busy."

Sam wasn't going to risk it. They slammed their palm down on the little brass bell until the woman at the desk covered the phone receiver and said in an irritated tone, "Yes?"

"I'm here to pick up my birth certificate?" I didn't mean for it to come out sounding so unsure.

"You'll need to fill out a request form and wait forty-eight hours," said the woman. "The fee is twenty-five dollars, and we don't take checks." She started to turn back to her conversation.

"I already filled out the form," I said. "I got a call a few days ago saying it was ready. I just haven't had time to come in and pick it up until now."

She wrinkled her nose, sighed, and finally set the phone aside. "Your name, please?"

"Callie Hart."

"Your *full* name?"

I hesitated. "That's it. It's not short for anything."

She huffed and pushed up out of her chair. "Just a moment."

While we waited for her to return with the envelope, I paced. I couldn't help myself. My hip felt annoyingly empty. I wished I'd brought my gun; I'd feel safer. More secure. Not that they'd have let me bring it in the building. Ohio might've had lax open-carry laws, but even they didn't let you bring a weapon into a public building without a special permit, and I didn't have one. Not even bodyguards got to break that rule.

"Callie Hart?" The woman at the desk called my name as if there were dozens waiting in the tiny lobby.

I looked around. We were the only ones. I wasn't going to argue with her, though. At least she had what I'd come for. My hopes that I wouldn't be able to get it dashed, I grabbed the envelope, paid the fee, and made for the door.

Sam ran to catch up with me. "You're not going to open it?"

I shook my head. "Not now. It's not the right time."

"Is there ever going to *be* a right time?"

I halted in the hallway next to a sign with detailed instructions on hand-washing. "Look, Sam. I'm just not ready. I know you mean well, but please just give me at least a few hours, okay?"

"Of course, Callie." Sam offered their pinky. "As long as

you pinky-swear to open it before we get on the plane home."

I looked at their pinky, just hanging there in the air, waiting for me to wrap mine around it and say the words. A pinky-swear didn't use to be a big thing between friends, but now that I knew I was half-fae, my promises felt like they had more weight. Nothing had changed—I was still me in all the ways that counted—yet everything had. I had magic now, and there was no telling how binding my promises might be now that my power had awakened.

What was the harm in a little pinky-swear, though?

I hooked my pinky around theirs, and we shook on it. "Deal."

We walked back to the car.

"This time, I'm driving," I said, holding out my hand for Sam to toss me the keys.

"No problemo." Sam pitched the keys over the roof of the car.

I caught them with ease, unlocked the door, and climbed in. I was just getting ready to buckle my seatbelt when the back door opened and Vaughn Meyer slid into the back seat.

I twisted around to look at him. "What the hell are you doing in my car?

The vampire smirked, showing off his fangs. "I am here to talk. Before you choose to act, know that I am armed and will defend myself if necessary."

"So are we," Sam shot back and yanked their parking pass down from the mirror.

I facepalmed and shook my head.

Sam stared at the scarlet and gray pass in their hand

and tossed it on the dash. "I meant Callie has magic. She'll freeze your ass and shatter you into a million pieces before you can say what's up."

"She'll do no such thing." Vaughn's eyes slid to me as he adjusted his suit jacket. "I am here to have a conversation and to pass along an olive branch, nothing more."

"You could've just knocked on my door," I ground out.

Vaughn raised an eyebrow. "And you would've invited me in for tea?"

Good point. I would've told him to kiss my ass and called down to building security to have him removed.

He leaned forward, sticking his head between our seats. "I think this is a conversation best had in motion, especially since we both have places to be. I suggest you drive."

Driving away with a vampire in the back seat was the last thing I wanted to do, but I didn't have much choice. I couldn't toss magic around in the car, not with Sam sitting right there. They could get hurt. Besides, Vaughn was a slimy bastard, but if he said he wanted to have a business talk, I believed him. Ripping open our throats in a moving vehicle wasn't his style.

I started the car and pulled out of the parking lot, easing onto the freeway. "Where to?"

"Just drive until I tell you otherwise," he said, "but keep to the right. This conversation won't take long."

I stayed in the second lane from the right and adjusted the mirror so I could keep a better eye on him as we moved along the highway. Traffic wasn't bad, but then again, it was Monday afternoon.

"So, what do you want?" I asked the vampire.

Vaughn leaned back in the seat, making himself

comfortable. "First, I need to know what was said to Queen Mab about me."

"About you specifically? Or vampires in general?"

He narrowed his eyes. "Do not toy with me, Ms. Hart. You know exactly what I mean. Should I be expecting Queen Mab's forces to mobilize?"

I knew I was right about his involvement with Jax. "No, not this time. But don't go thinking I'll cover for you every time you try to start a war. I don't want there to be a war between fae and vampires, but I'm not going to cover for you."

"Nor do I expect you to." He folded his arms.

I glanced into the rearview mirror. "I'm on to you, you know, and so is Ronan. Whatever it is you're up to, you're not going to get away with it."

"If I wanted to start something, I would, and there would be nothing you could do to stop me. Not you, not Ronan, not Queen Mab. I do not answer to you."

"But you do answer to the vampire aristocracy." Sam raised a finger.

Vaughn frowned. "How much does she know?"

"It's they or them," Sam corrected. "And for your information, I know everything."

"Only because you went snooping," I added. "And as for you, Vaughn, I stopped you once before. I'll do it again if I have to."

Our eyes met in the rearview mirror.

Vaughn was the first to look away, redirecting his gaze out the window at the passing cars. "Take the ramp for downtown and pull over in front of the capitol building. I have business there."

I flipped on the turn signal and slid into the next lane. The exit came up on the right, and I couldn't take it fast enough. "You said you were here to extend an olive branch. How do you intend to do that? And do you really expect Ronan to forgive you for trying to assassinate him?"

Vaughn smoothed his hands across his chest. "An olive branch means the restoration of friendly relations. It is not an apology, nor is it an admission of guilt. It simply means that I am willing to extend a gesture of goodwill in order to restore working relationships."

Sam snorted. "In other words, no."

I pulled up in front of the capitol, a large, sprawling white building with columns and a huge dome. "In any case, what is this olive branch of yours?"

Vaughn brought his briefcase up onto his lap and flipped it open. A moment later, he was holding a manila envelope out to me that looked identical to the one I'd just gotten at the vital statistics office. "Please see to it that Ronan gets this." He threw open the door and placed one foot on the sidewalk before hesitating and turning back to me with a smile. "Have a nice day, Ms. Hart. Enjoy your vacation. I hear France is very nice this time of year, although a bit chilly and sadly lacking in beaches." With that, he exited the car.

"France?" Sam asked, wrinkling their nose. "Tells you what he knows. We're going to Spain, not France. Although I've always wanted to see Paris."

"It looks like you might have your chance," I said, peeking into the envelope. I opened it the rest of the way and brought out an ornate invitation on thick paper. "You and a guest are cordially invited to attend the annual celebration of the signing of the peace accords to be held this weekend in Paris, France at *Le Bristol*."

"But we can't go to France! We've already got reservations in Spain!"

I stuffed the paper back into the envelope and dropped it beside my seat, right next to the birth certificate envelope. "This is just another one of Vaughn's games. I'm sure Ronan won't want to go either. I've never seen the man turn down an opportunity to work." *Or to let beautiful women gawk at him,* I thought, and eased out into traffic.

Ronan wasn't going to miss those photoshoots, certainly not over an invitation to some fancy celebration where he'd have to be seen acting as a liaison for his mother's court. If there was one thing he hated more than fae court politics, it was his mother.

CHAPTER TWO

After two days off and my latest encounter with Vaughn Meyer, it was a relief to see Ronan's house. There was something to be said for routine. I liked the surety of my job, of always knowing who was coming and going and why. Sam and Ronan thought it was because I was a control freak. I was anything but. If I hadn't paid such close attention all the time, they'd both be dead by now.

I got out of the car and opened the back to help Sam with their bags. I'd managed to cram a week's worth of travel clothes and supplies into a single suitcase, and one garment bag held an extra work suit. Sam, however, had brought double everything I did. Sam was practically two people shoved into one body. Sometimes, they'd be the most feminine person I knew, complete with pink hair, pink dresses, and perfect makeup. The next day, Sam would decide to rock a suit and tie. They looked good in both, but sometimes I wished they would just pick a single style of dress and stick to it. Hauling two suitcases and two garment bags plus a backpack full of art equipment up the stairs to Ronan's front door wore me out.

Sam put down the laptop bag they'd brought up the stairs and pretended to wipe sweat off their forehead. "Don't forget your birth certificate, Callie. Oh, and the party invitation."

The door opened at the wrong time, and Ronan asked, "What party invitation?"

I cringed. I'd been hoping I could say I forgot both. I didn't think Ronan would decide to attend the party, but on the off chance that he would, we could avoid the whole thing by just leaving the invitation in the car. I could always say I forgot, or pretend Vaughn had not given it to me.

"I'll be right back." I groaned and trudged down the stairs one more time to retrieve both envelopes.

By the time I returned to the front door, Ronan had picked up two of Sam's suitcases, and they were busy hauling it all inside. The envelopes seemed all but forgotten, so I put them on a side table, hoping they were.

"I'm looking forward to getting some sun," Ronan said. "I don't mind Ohio most of the year, but these gray skies are really getting to me. I normally have more photoshoots out west by this time of year, but things seem to have scaled back. There are too many fashion magazines and ads reusing the same pictures, with a little Photoshop thrown in. I'm lucky I don't need the money. Work is getting scarce."

"Poor little rich boy," I teased, dragging the last suitcases in. "Oh, whatever will you do?"

"Might have to pick a nice street corner to play on," he

mused. "Do you think we could get the piano down there? Or would that be too much?"

"You haven't replaced your electric violin yet?" Sam asked.

"I was planning on shopping for one while we were in Spain." Ronan dropped the last suitcase with a thud. "No offense, Sam, but what do you have in here? Bricks?"

"That's my accessories bag." Sam picked the bag up and leaned it against the others.

Ronan sighed and rubbed his forehead. "I guess we're lucky to have a private jet. This would be costing a fortune in baggage fees alone otherwise. So, did you two finish making out your itinerary?"

"We did," Sam said, "but there's something you should see."

I tried elbowing Sam in the ribs, but they slipped away and stuck their tongue out at me from afar.

Ronan turned to me. "Guess this is the party invitation you were talking about. What's all that about?"

I sighed and grabbed the envelopes from where I'd left them on a table near the door. "We ran into Vaughn Meyer today," I said, holding one of them out to him.

Ronan took the envelope, opened it, and took out the document inside, scanning it quickly. He frowned. "Callie, this isn't a party invitation. This is your birth certificate."

My heart jumped into my throat. I grabbed the envelope from him and shook the paper back inside without looking at it. "My mistake," I said, holding out the other envelope. "This is the one you want."

Ronan's fingers closed around it. "Have you looked at that yet?" He nodded to the birth certificate envelope.

"She's waiting for the right time." Sam crossed their arms and leaned against the wall. "Personally, I think Callie's just stalling, though for the life of me I can't figure out why. Don't you want to know who your family is? Where they are?"

I did, or at least, I thought I did. There was some part of me that believed everything would change once I had that information. I had a vision in my head of who I was, and I didn't want some name on a piece of paper to change that. It didn't have to, and I knew that too, but I couldn't shake the strange anxiety I had concerning my birth certificate.

It wasn't like the names on it were going to tell me everything I needed to know about being half-fae. It wouldn't even tell me which court my mother or father had belonged to. All I would find were their names. It would tell me nothing about their personalities, their history, or their lives. It most certainly wouldn't tell me why they had given me away and condemned me to a miserable childhood in the foster care system.

I shrugged. "Of course I do. It's just not the most important thing in my life right now. It can wait, unlike us, if we want to make that departure time, right, Ronan?"

He looked up from the invitation he'd been reading, his face sprouting a smile. "Absolutely."

"So, we won't be adjusting our plans to include a trip to Paris?" Sam asked.

Ronan shoved the invitation back into the envelope and tossed it on a nearby chair. "No, I don't believe we will."

A sudden knock on the door interrupted us. I was just about to turn and open it when the knob turned of its own accord and the door swung open. A woman in a long flowing blue dress floated into the room like a storm, her glass shoes clicking on the floor. She wore her blonde hair piled atop her head beneath a crown of ice. Despite the relative warmth of the air outside, she wore a cloak of fuzzy white.

"When are you going to give me a key, dear son?" Queen Mab of the winter court asked.

"The day after never," Ronan replied dryly. "Why give you a key when you can just open the door and invite yourself in anytime you like?"

Mab pressed her lips together and looked around. "True. Ah, Callie, my dear! There you are!"

I wanted to vomit at the sound of her forcing herself to be nice to me. We didn't see eye to eye, the queen and me. The only reason she'd been pleasant to me over the last month was that she wanted me to join her court and add my powers to hers or something like that.

"Don't look so moody, Callie," the queen said and clapped her hands. "I come with a gift." A velvet-lined rectangular box appeared in her hand that she held out to me.

I sighed and took the box, opening it to reveal a stunning, diamond-studded gold necklace. The thing had to be worth a fortune. I glanced up from the box, meeting Mab's expectant gaze. "You know you're not allowed to bribe me into choosing your court, right?"

"Don't be ridiculous!" She gave a nervous chuckle and waved a dismissive hand. "That would be against fae law! No, this is just...a token of my appreciation. For what you did last month for Ronan. I thought you could stand to spruce up your wardrobe a bit. It is rather...pedestrian.

What's all this?" She gestured to the suitcases lying around.

"We're preparing for an extended trip to Spain, mother. I told you about that last week." Ronan crossed his arms.

"Oh, no, no, no! Spain? That won't do it all! You can't be in two places at once! How will you attend the peace gathering in Paris if you're in Spain?"

Ronan and I exchanged glances.

I mimicked his crossed arm stance, moving to stand next to him. "We're not going to Paris."

She puffed up like an angry chicken. "It's not up to you!" The queen turned to her son, taking a step forward. "We discussed this last year, Ronan. I agreed to go to last year's celebration so you could attend a photoshoot in Japan. In exchange, you were to go this year. Surely you haven't forgotten?"

He sighed and turned his head away, muttering a mild curse.

I lowered my arms. I could've throttled him. "You forgot, didn't you?"

"It's been a very long year, Callie. Mother, I can't go. I have *work*."

"Work you don't need." She gestured around the foyer of his mansion. "I provide everything you could want. Any lost income will be seen to."

Ronan nodded. "Maybe you can replace my income and maintain whatever lifestyle I choose, but I can't just cancel gigs whenever I want, Mother. It hurts my reputation. In this industry—"

Mab clenched her fists and stood up taller, her voice booming like thunder. "You will go to the peace celebration in Paris, Ronan, and you will be seen there. That is an order from your queen! And if you refuse me again," she said, sticking her pointer finger in Ronan's face, "I will have my knight escort you to Paris, and you'll spend the entire event under his guard!"

Whatever rebuttal Ronan had prepared, he dropped it immediately at the mention of the winter knight. His shoulders slumped, and he sighed.

Mab took her son's chin in her hands, smiling sympathetically. "Don't be glum, son. At least your bags are already packed." She took a step back toward the door. "I'll take care of all the travel arrangements. Do call me once you've landed, so I know you've arrived safely!"

And just like that, Mab fled the house as quickly as she'd come.

Sam's suitcase fell over.

I frowned, staring at the closed front door. "Well, damn. There goes Spain."

"It's not all bad," said Sam, picking up the suitcase. "I mean, we get to go to Paris. The City of Lovers." They wiggled their eyebrows.

I shot Sam a warning glare.

"And art museums." Ronan picked up a bag and slung it over his shoulder with a sigh. "No beaches, though. And here I was looking forward to babes in bikinis."

I made a gagging sound and picked up two bags to haul to the car so we could get to the airport faster.

CHAPTER THREE

I sat in the back of the cabin near the bar with my feet propped up on the seat across from me, phone in hand. Mab had had the decency to email me a list of attendees for the event, as well as the dossiers she kept on the guests. Most of the information in the dossier had been blacked out or redacted, but there was enough information in each file to give me some idea of who was who.

In addition to our party of three, the summer fae were sending a delegation, or rather a delegate—a person named Kai Palakiko. Almost everything in his file had been removed, but from what I could tell, he was the summer knight. For a moment, I wondered why Mab didn't just send her knight, and then I remembered he was a masked terror. Probably not the jolly sort. Ronan would be a better, friendlier ambassador, one all the ladies at the event would fall all over themselves to look at. Just as our flight attendant was currently doing.

I lowered my phone and squinted my eyes at the tall brunette as she laughed at one of his stupid jokes. It couldn't possibly be that funny. She'd been hovering over him ever since takeoff, bringing him drinks and snacks and smiling like an idiot. I glanced at the empty Coke can next to me. Here we were, four hours into an eleven-hour flight, and I had yet to get a refill.

One of the new hires we'd brought on the trip with us entered the main cabin from the rear and stopped next to the bar. He stood in front of the fridge a minute before running his hands through a head of short, spiky brown hair and glancing over at me.

I buried myself in my manual, pretending to be busy. *Please don't come over and talk to me.*

A moment later, he was next to me, holding out an ice-cold can of Coke and smiling. "You looked like you could use a top-off."

I couldn't very well refuse a drink after I'd just glared at the flight attendant for not bringing me one, now could I? "Thanks." I took the can and placed it in the empty cup holder next to me. I waited for him to move on, but he just stood there awkwardly, expecting me to invite him to sit. "It's Mark, isn't it?" I took my feet off the seat and gestured to it.

He sat excitedly, leaning forward on the edge of the seat with his palms resting on his knees. "Yes, ma'am."

"There's no need to call me ma'am."

"Sorry, boss." He hesitated. "Is that okay?"

I lowered the phone. Mark was one of the new guys. Ronan hadn't wanted to hire more people for my security team, but after David broke his wrist fighting Jax and I'd had to leave him twice during pursuits, we didn't have much choice. Plus, we needed more staff to cover vacations, time off, and so on. At least three other people had to be working full-time hours so I could take a day off every once in a while, so given people's proclivities to get sick or go on vacation, we'd hired four more full-time guards. We'd brought three of the new people and left the remaining part-timer and the other new guy home to mind the house.

Mark had familiar credentials. Military background, worked part-time at a security firm in civilian life...and he was half-fae. I'd hired him as much for that last reason as any other. Being half-fae myself, I wanted to see how he'd adjusted to his life in the winter court. Of course, unlike me, Mark had grown up with that connection. I still wanted to make sure they didn't treat him differently because he was only half-fae.

There was just one problem with Mark. He flinched at loud noises and constantly asked if he was doing things right, even when it was clear to anyone he was. We had a word for guys like that in the service, but it wasn't a polite one. In security, I stuck to calling him gun-shy. The kid wasn't meant for any job where he was going to get shot at or jumped by vampires. He'd thrown up every time we hit turbulence. I'd been trying to think of a nice way to fire him, but I liked him too much for that. He was nice, even if he was a bit clingy.

"You can just call me Callie." I put the phone away. "What's on your mind, Mark?"

He fidgeted with his thumbs, staring at his hands. "I was wondering about the sudden change in plans. Have you had time to go over the floor plans and the guest list? Do you know where we'll be staying?"

"I forwarded all that information to your email."

"Oh, right. I forgot." He sat there silently for a moment. Mark didn't even reach for his phone.

I cleared my throat. "Is there something else, Mark?"

"Yeah, actually." He scooted further toward the edge of his seat. "I wanted to thank you for giving me a chance with this job. I know I'm not the most intimidating person. Without a gun, I'm practically useless in a fight. My strength's always been in seeing things other people don't. Attention to detail. My mom says I'm good at that, and security is a good fit for someone like me."

I cringed inwardly. Now I'd never be able to fire him. Best I could hope for would be to discourage him subtly. Maybe he'd move on and find other work where he'd be safer. "Being a bodyguard isn't quite the same thing. When I leave Ronan in your hands, it's a very real possibility that maybe someday you'll have to shoot someone."

"I know." He sat up straighter. "I can do that. I proved that before, didn't I?"

He had. The kid might not have been much of a fighter, but he was an expert marksman if you gave him enough time to line up a shot. If he'd been a little more callous and a lot less jumpy, the military could've used a sniper like him. In a real firefight, though, I didn't think he'd get off a shot. He took an impossible amount of time to get his sights lined up, even if he hit every bullseye.

"You might have to act fast," I continued. "Vampires are fast."

"Ideally, though, shouldn't our goal be to keep Ronan from being in a situation where I have to shoot? If I'm paying attention, I should be able to head off any potential threats, right?"

He had me there. "That's true most of the time, but what about the threats you don't see coming? Everyone makes mistakes, Mark. Even me."

"I'll try not to."

See what I mean? How do you dislike a guy who tries so hard?

I sighed and decided it was best to change the subject. "Did you want to go over the floor plans together?"

He nodded emphatically and fished out his phone. "Jim and Yvonne are asleep right now. I figure we'll go over them again before we check in."

I hadn't planned on looking at the hotel floor plans or going over shifts until after we arrived. I wanted to do a full security briefing. But since this was Mark, and he asked, I figured it wouldn't hurt to go over it one on one with him.

The hotel was some high-end place, one of the best in Paris. Ronan had been given a two-bedroom suite. As head of security, I took the second bedroom, which I was going to share with Sam. The three other security staff members had their own suite down the hall, giving us the entire floor. I'd decided to run everyone in staggered six-hour rotations, which should keep everyone from getting exhausted. I wanted my team sharp and ready for any threats. We were heading into an unfamiliar city and expecting close contact with vampires. Anything could happen.

"What exactly can we expect during the party?" Mark asked.

I frowned and looked past him to where Ronan sat, still flirting with our flight attendant. "I'm not sure. I was just going to go ask him. Why don't you go back to the others and see if you can work out between you who's going to take what shifts? You can wait until they wake up, as long as it's settled before we land. I'll make any adjustments based on your agreement."

Mark nodded and rose from his seat.

I breathed a sigh of relief. I liked him, but it could be draining. I waited to make sure he had gone to the rear of the plane before I got out of my seat and went to interrupt Ronan's flirting.

The flight attendant gave a loud, nasal laugh as I approached and slapped the armrest before reaching to cover her nose.

I faked a laugh and clapped Ronan on the back. "This guy's hilarious! Am I right? Hey, I think I heard the people in the back needed something."

"Oh, the bar's open. Feel free to take whatever you need." She tried to turn her attention back to Ronan.

"He was really insistent. You might want to go check it out."

"Sorry, we'll have to catch up later. Don't let her work you too hard," she said, gesturing to me. "You need your beauty sleep." The flight attendant put her hand on his arm as she walked by, and something in me wanted to clock her right in that upturned nose.

"What is this? Flirt-with-Every-Skirt-You-See Day?" I grumbled as I dropped into the chair across from him.

Ronan leaned on his fist, regarding me from behind half-lidded eyes. "It was just a little harmless flirting. I'm bored, the trip is long, and I haven't been on a proper date in two months unless you count the few times I took you out."

"Those weren't dates."

"A fact you continue to remind me of." He sat up and stretched. "I think you're impervious to flirtation, Callie Hart. I pity the man who tries to climb into your bed. He might get something important frozen off."

"What's that supposed to mean?" I crossed my arms.

"It means you'd fit right in with the winter court. You can be as cold and callous as anyone there. Every woman who's come near me in the last month, you scare off."

"That last one had a criminal record. Prostitution, Ronan."

"How was I supposed to know?" He shrugged.

"I don't know, have some standards, maybe? Or at least raise them. 'Bimbo with a booty' isn't enough of a qualification. I'm sorry, but she was a security risk. You hired me to keep you safe. I can't and won't keep protecting you from venereal disease."

He turned his head, focusing out the window to the passing clouds. "I guess I'm just lonely."

The way he said it almost made me feel bad for him. It had to be hard on him, always being around people, but never getting close to anyone. He was always shuffling from one location to the next. The only people he had constant contact with was his staff, and he generally maintained a friendly but professional relationship with them. Of everyone, we probably spent the most time together, but that was part of the job. I'd never seen him invite friends over, and the few women he had been involved with had been quick flings during a stopover in another city.

I sighed and relaxed into my seat. "Don't take this the wrong way, Ronan, but maybe you should consider making some friends to fill your time."

"When? And what sort of people would I make friends with? My co-workers? You've met people in the industry, Callie." He tilted his head, giving me a doubtful look.

I had. One of his most recent gigs had been booked back to back against two others, meaning there were three models in the same dressing room at the same time, each waiting to be called for their shoot. The egos in that room would've made the *Titanic* look small by comparison, Ronan's included. They spent much of their free time on their phones, hate-liking each other's social media photos. When they weren't ignoring each other outright, they'd fake-smile at each other and offer compliments that were cleverly disguised insults. They were probably the least friendly co-workers I'd ever seen. He had a point.

Then there were the photographers and their assistants. Some of them had been friendly, but most of them were just interested in doing their work and moving on to the next thing. No one took the time to chat with anyone about their personal life.

Ronan had his music hobby, but that was something he did alone.

"Maybe you should join an orchestra or something," I suggested. "Or you could host a dinner party and invite people over."

"I don't have the time to dedicate to an orchestra. That'd be a full-time job. As for dinner parties, how many do you think I could get away with before my mother scared them all away?" He sighed and rested his chin on his fist.

"Maybe if you'd quit feeling sorry for yourself and tell your mother to back off, you wouldn't *be* so isolated." I hadn't meant for that to slip out, but I was getting frustrated with him. He always had an excuse for why he was miserable. In the end, it always seemed to boil down to his mother. Ronan was a grown man who should've been able to do what he wanted when he wanted. Instead, he'd let his mother derail his entire life.

Ronan lowered his arm and looked at me, his expression unreadable.

Well, I've already put my foot in my mouth. Might as well keep going. "I understand she's more than your mother, she's your queen. But between you and me, she's nosy and rude. She's going to keep inserting herself into your life, keep pushing you, keep running everything and ruining it until you put your foot down."

"You're absolutely right," he said, nodding emphatically. "You know what, this whole summit is going to be boring. I do have to make an appearance, but nobody specified how long I had to be there. Once I'm seen and meet all the required people, why don't we get right back on the plane and see if we can salvage some of our week in Spain?"

"That's the spirit!" I pumped a fist and smiled.

"If I play my cards right, I could get lucky in two different countries in one week."

I lowered my excited fist, and the smile dropped from my face. That was a lot less exciting to hear. "Did you hear nothing I said? We just finished going over how random hookups are a security risk."

He grinned and waved a hand. "Relax, Callie. This was supposed to be a vacation before my mother wrecked it, remember? It's supposed to be *fun*. I'm starting to think you don't know what that word means."

"I know how to have fun." I sat up straighter and worked to keep my voice from going too high, so I didn't sound defensive.

"Oh, really? What was the last thing you did for fun?" Ronan crossed his arms, waiting.

"I… Well, last week I—"

His eyebrows shot up in disbelief. "Last week? Callie, that's not living. Admit it; you're a workaholic."

"I am not! You're only saying that because the only time you see me is at work."

"Yeah," he scoffed, "but whose fault is that? I asked you to go to dinner with me three weeks ago to pay off my debt, and you know what you said? You said you were *busy*. On your day off."

"That was three weeks ago!"

"And it was probably the last time anyone asked you out, wasn't it? Besides, three weeks isn't that long."

I clenched my hands into fists, genuinely annoyed by how hard he was digging at me, and what I chose to do in my personal time. "We've known each other a month. That means it was over seventy-five percent of our relationship ago. Practically a lifetime if you look at it in dog years."

"Dog years?" He squinted at me. "I thought that was seven times human years, not ten."

"I don't know!" I threw my hands up and stood

abruptly. "I was a grunt, Ronan, not a math major! You want a bodyguard who can do calculus, you should've gotten yourself a flyboy. They do math. I point and shoot. See the difference?"

"That's why I hired you. I don't need—"

"Then let me do my damn job and listen to me for once!"

Ronan stood much more slowly and calmly than I had. For the first time since I'd met him, I watched anger flash behind his blue eyes. "I'm not trying to tell you how to do your job," he said, his tone chillingly even. "I'm trying to tell you that you're of no use to me if you work yourself to death. You want to be good at what you do? Then learn to relax in your off time. Take up a hobby. Live. Because if you keep going at this rate, you'll burn out. A year from now, you're going to hate your work, and you're going to hate me. That's the last thing I want!"

"Ladies!" Sam appeared in the narrow space between us, pushing us apart. "I'm not saying we can't settle this without an all-out brawl, but maybe if you're going to punch each other, wait until we're not thirty thousand feet in the air over the Atlantic Ocean, huh?"

I shot Sam a warning glare. "Nobody's punching anybody."

"I can't tell half the time if you two want to hit each other or bone," they said, crossing their arms and taking a tentative step back.

Ronan and I looked at each other.

"Either way," Sam continued, "some of us are trying to sleep so we can enjoy Paris, so whatever you're going to do, kindly get a room."

"I think I'll just go back to my seat," I said, tugging down my shirt. "I've said everything relevant, anyway."

Sam raised their arms and eyes to the ceiling. "Hallelujah."

I slunk to the rear of the cabin and slid into a seat as far from Ronan as I could get. We were going to be spending plenty of time together over the next few days, trapped in a hotel room together. Might as well enjoy what little alone time I had while I had it.

CHAPTER FOUR

The plane landed in Paris around ten a.m. local time. I didn't sleep enough during the flight, which left me exhausted. We disembarked and piled our luggage in one spot, waiting for the limo we'd hired to come and get us.

Several cars pulled up a short while later, but not the one Mab had hired. These were full of vampires. I inched closer to Ronan as they piled out of the cars, suddenly feeling underdressed in my travel clothes. The woman who approached us wore a flawless pantsuit and had every hair in place, tucked into a tight bun. I recognized her from the dossier Mab had given us.

She smiled, exposing her fangs, and extended a hand to Ronan. "Welcome," she said in French. "My name is Natalie. You must be Ronan McCalister."

"That's me," Ronan replied, also in French.

My French wasn't great, but I'd retained a smattering from high school. As long as we stuck to basic conversation, I would be fine, but anything more complex and I'd be lost.

Ronan gestured to me and thankfully added in English, "This is Callie Hart, my head of security, and my friend, Sam Shoemaker."

We shook hands. Her fingers were cold to the touch, and I had to fight to keep from shivering. Sam wasn't so good at hiding it. They shuddered and shrank into the background.

"It's good to meet you," Natalie said in heavily accented English. "I've heard so much about you."

"About me?" I looked at Ronan, who shrugged.

"Of course. Perhaps I should explain. You know Vaughn Meyer, yes?"

"Yes, I know him," I ground out through clenched teeth.

Natalie didn't seem to notice. She just kept on smiling. "Yes, he and I have been in close contact throughout the years. He is a good friend. He told me what a capable and strong young woman you are. I can tell from your hand-shake that he was telling the truth."

I'll bet he did. I had to bite my lip to keep from muttering that out loud.

Natalie turned to Ronan, her expression growing more somber. "I was disappointed to hear that Queen Mab wouldn't be joining us."

"Yes, unfortunately, my mother is tied up in the usual affairs of state. I hope I'm able to fill in for her." Had Ronan been practicing that line? It sounded almost scripted, as if he'd spewed the answer on automatic. Maybe he had. From the sounds of it, he filled in for her on a semi-regular basis whenever she had obligations outside Faerie.

"Don't be ridiculous." Natalie let out a high-pitched laugh and dismissed Ronan's doubts with a wave of her hand. "I'm so glad you could join us. Your presence is more than welcome. Please, I have made arrangements to see you to the hotel. My people will take your bags."

Ronan seemed willing to just let them take our stuff, but I stepped forward. "We wouldn't want to impose."

"Oh, it's not an imposition. Not at all!" Natalie smiled as several men in black suits stepped away from her car to retrieve our bags. She folded her hands in front of her. "We want you to be comfortable and to feel safe while you're here with us. I realize you've brought your security team, and that's perfectly fine so long as they're willing to coordinate with the venue's security. I'd like for everyone to be on the same page."

"Absolutely," I replied, though inside I was screaming. This was going to be a nightmare. I just knew it.

Natalie's smile widened. "Wonderful! Please, this way. The summer delegate has already arrived. You can ride together."

I gestured to the three guards we'd brought with us—Jim, Yvonne, and Mark—to take the rear car along with our bags. Hopefully, they were smart enough to ensure the vampires didn't go digging through our things. Not that we had brought anything with us that would cause trouble. I'd ensured that by checking everyone's bags before takeoff. Still, I didn't like the idea of vampires touching my stuff. I was sure Ronan wouldn't like it either.

Sam, Ronan, and I followed Natalie to the front car, in which she'd indicated the summer court delegate was waiting. I didn't see him until I'd already ducked into the car and settled in my seat. He'd tucked himself against the far door, looking so comfortable he'd almost melted into the seat.

When I'd read Kai's dossier on the plane, it had included a photo, so I knew what he was supposed to look like. The picture, however, didn't do him justice. Kai Palakiko was the sort of attractive man who graced calendars and romcom movie posters. Ronan might have been a model, and he wasn't hard to look at by any means, but there was a difference between being photogenic and being drop-dead gorgeous.

Sam slid into the seat next to Kai, staring at him with wide eyes.

Kai's bright smile lit up the car as we entered, and he sat forward. "Ronan! It's been a while!"

Ronan acknowledged him with a grunt and a nod. "Kai."

"I'm Sam," Sam said, beaming at Kai. They put out a fist for a bump rather than shake hands.

Kai grinned and obliged. "Very pleased to meet you, Sam. And who's this? I hadn't heard you had a girlfriend." He gestured to me.

"Oh, she's not—"

"Callie Hart," I said, extending my hand. "I work for Ronan. Security."

"My mistake." Kai wrapped both hands around mine and lifted the back of my hand to his lips. "Ronan has a habit of surrounding himself with pretty things. I should have known better than to assume you were just another pretty thing in his collection."

My cheeks warmed. I retracted my hand and cleared my throat. "Funny you should mention that."

"Of course," said Kai, throwing one arm behind the seat and relaxing again, "it's a problem, isn't it? So many pretty things, so many of us collectors. Eventually, we'll all just start collecting ourselves. Narcissus, pool. You understand."

I frowned. "Actually, that one's lost on me."

"Narcissus was the jerk son of a god in Greek mythology," Ronan explained with a harsh smile, glaring at Kai. "He was beautiful, and almost everyone who met him fell instantly in love with him and his beauty, but no one loved Narcissus more than he himself did. He saw his reflection in a pool and fell in love with it. When he realized what he'd done, he committed suicide."

"It's where the word 'narcissist' comes from." Kai lifted his hand and pretended to be examining his fingernails. "We're all a little narcissistic is what I was saying. Some of us more than others."

"If you've got something to say…" Ronan started.

I glanced at them. They seemed to be having a conversation on another level, one I wasn't privy to. They've probably got history, I thought. Of course, they would. Ronan knew a lot of people in the fae world, and in both courts. Kai was the summer knight. They'd obviously met before. Maybe it hadn't gone so well.

Kai pressed his lips together and shrugged. "No, not really. I just think people should share their things instead of hoarding them, and that true beauty can be found in the most mundane of places."

I decided they were probably posturing. That was what happened when you put two men in a closed space together. They beat their chests and threw leaves until they figured out which of them was going to be the head ape during all future interactions. Kai wasn't a security threat as far as I could tell, so I focused my attention out the window.

I'd never seen Paris, outside of the photographs I'd come across online. It was a city both strange and beautiful, where the ancient blended seamlessly with the modern. Cathedrals that had stood for centuries were right at home next to modern banks, for example. Bright red and green cloth hung over the entrances to cafes and bakeries, while decorative tables sat empty out front. The weather wasn't bad, but it wasn't great either. Gray clouds hung over the city, blocking out the sun and threatening rain. It wasn't cold, but it wasn't warm. Aside from the unique architecture and the foreign language, it felt like I'd never left Ohio.

"I like Paris," Kai was saying, "I just wish they would hold these celebrations somewhere...more temperate. I miss the sun already."

"Tell me about it." Sam rolled their eyes. "I'm not sure I even remember what a sunny day looks like. We're from Ohio, the land of no sun in the fall, winter, or spring. We get one or two good months of it. The last month is dedicated to rain."

"Ah!" Kai nodded sympathetically. "You should move to Hawaii. Two hundred seventy-one sunny days a year, clean ocean air, beautiful people, beautiful culture... In fact, I think I'll petition to have the event moved there next year."

Ronan crossed his arms. "It's held in Paris because this is neutral ground. They'll never agree to move it to Hawaii. That's considered part of your queen's kingdom."

Kai conceded the point with a shrug. "True, but at least

they could hold it in the warmer months, eh? We could all do with a little sun. Well, except maybe the vampires."

I couldn't help but laugh along with Kai and Sam.

Ronan was the only sour one in the car. He lowered his chin and muttered, "That's just in the movies. They don't burst into flame in the sunlight. Everybody knows that."

"Lighten up." I elbowed him in the ribs. "Never thought I'd have to say that to you."

"Yes, where's the genial Prince Ronan, the light of the winter court?" Kai folded his hands and leaned forward. "I remember you being much more energetic, friend."

"We aren't friends," Ronan snapped back. "Callie, don't forget who you're laughing and talking with. This man is the summer knight. He may seem funny, but he didn't get his position by cracking jokes."

Kai grinned. "You're right. I didn't. I got here because I can hold my own in a fight, which is why I don't need a bodyguard."

"Do you want to fight me?" Ronan asked, sitting forward. "Name the time and place."

"I don't think that's a good idea." I put my hand on Ronan's arm and eased him back in the seat. "This is supposed to be a peace celebration. What will the vampires think if two fae fight each other?"

Kai shrugged. "I don't want to fight you. Summer and winter have no quarrel with each other these days, and I have nothing to prove. Can you say the same?"

Ronan was so angry, he was practically steaming. What was it with them?

The car stopped, and not a moment too soon. I thought I was going to have to break up a fight in the back seat if we drove much farther. The doors opened, and Sam scurried to get out. I waited for Ronan, who exited next.

"You should come to tea at the summer palace," Kai said before I could climb out of the car.

I looked around. "Me?"

"Of course. Who else would I be talking to? My queen would be delighted to meet you."

I glanced toward the door. Ronan was waiting for me on the other side, but he would keep for a minute. The other three guards were with him, and I had to trust they'd be able to do their jobs without me hovering over them all the time.

I shut the door. "Are you asking me because I'm an undecided fae and you want to win my allegiance for your court or because the queen would actually be delighted to meet me?"

Kai's laugh was smooth and easy. "A little of both, probably. Although it's against fae law to entice you, I don't think tea and cookies count as a bribe. You should be able to make an informed decision, Callie. I know you've already seen what winter has to offer. Let us show you what waits for you in the summer court, should that be more to your liking."

I jumped when someone knocked on the window. Ronan opened the door a second later and poked his head in, frowning. "Everything okay in here?"

Kai placed a hand on my knee and winked at me before opening the opposite door. "Think about it. I'll drop by later to get your answer."

"What was that about?" Ronan asked once I got out of the car.

I adjusted my jacket. "I got invited to tea with the summer queen."

His frown deepened. "Be careful with him, Callie. Kai's a killer."

"So am I," I whispered back. "I think you're forgetting that."

"I haven't forgotten. I just don't want you to have to."

I looked up at the building before us, a huge white-painted structure with terraced windows, each boasting a flower box full of different-colored carnations. Le Bristol housed six stories of unequivocal luxury, according to the brochure I'd read. The hotel also housed an art gallery, a chocolatier, two restaurants, and a spa. It was a retreat within a retreat, the perfect place for the wealthy to get away from the busy streets of Paris.

Of course, people like Sam and me were much more interested in hitting the Paris streets, sampling the local cuisine, and taking in the local color. Paris wasn't my ideal spring destination, but I was there, and I wanted to enjoy the city at least a little bit while I could.

First, we had to get settled into our room.

The inside was even more elegant than the outside with wide-open spaces, polished floors, and upscale furniture arranged on oriental rugs. Tall windows let in natural light, the deep crimson curtains held back by golden ropes. Glass chandeliers hung from the ceiling, illuminating the buckets of red roses that had been placed on nearly every surface large enough to hold them.

On one side of the lobby was a huge painting that took up the whole wall, depicting some people dancing outside a house. They were dressed in clothes that might've been from the sixteenth or seventeenth century—I didn't know my French history well enough to be sure. Next to the painting stood the bust of some important person, marble, of course.

Everything was perfect, spotless, and probably cost more than I made in a year, even with what Ronan was paying me. In my frumpy, sweaty travel clothes, I felt very out of place. Sam, however, was beside themselves as they danced into the lobby, spinning and taking in the art culture, as they called it.

"Callie, look at this place!" Sam beamed as they rushed to look at the painting. "Wow, this is an original! All this stuff—it's beautiful! It's like I died and went to art heaven!"

I couldn't help but smile. "Just wait until we hit the galleries."

The hotel staff showed us to an elevator that went up to the fourth floor. The fourth floor in our wing housed only two suites, both of which would belong to us. Ronan, Sam, and I would take the larger of the two, while the three security staff would take the second. I swept our suite while Ronan and Sam stood in the hall with the rest of the security guards, then Mark stayed with them while I went with the other two to the security suite to make sure they had everything they needed.

Mark and the others inquired about coordinating with hotel security, as well as Natalie's event security, and I promised them I'd find out about that as soon as possible. We went over the shifts for the next twenty-four hours, made a few small adjustments, and reviewed protocol.

By the time I finally made it to our suite, our bags had arrived. Most of them were still piled in the middle of the living area, looking very out of place against the white carpet and white sofas. The only splashes of color in the room were the bright blue curtains and the dark stain on anything made of wood. It didn't look at all like a hotel room. Sam came out of one of the rooms.

"Callie!" They beamed. "You need to see this tub! You could fit a circus in there!"

I grabbed my bag from the pile and followed Sam back to the room, where I stood, stunned for a long moment, even though I'd seen it when I'd checked the suite. I'd expected a nice bed, a garden view, and a desk. That was all there, but there was an additional seating area away from the four-poster bed—three comfortable-looking armchairs arranged in a triangle. An extra desk had been tucked into the corner, and next to it sat a vanity. The dresser on the other side of the bed was bigger than the last boat I'd been in. Lastly, there was a plush blue loveseat. That was where Sam had tossed their stuffed owl and favorite blanket.

"Sam, you can sleep in the bed," I said, hauling my bag to the dresser. The bed was big enough that the two of us and our extended families could fit without touching.

"I know, but I don't want to keep you awake. I'm a wiggleworm." They picked up their stuffed owl, fluffed it, and placed it back on the loveseat. "Besides, you're working. You need your sleep more than me. I plan to be out as much as possible, enjoying the city."

All good points. I'd shared a bed with Sam only once, when we went to Cleveland and got stuck there due to snow. We'd had to crash at a seedy motel, and I wound up getting pushed out of bed. Sam couldn't lay still to save their life, not even when they were asleep.

"Well, if you change your mind, you're welcome to it," I reminded them.

"Oh, the bathroom!" Sam ran to a closed door and threw it open. "Look!"

I abandoned my bag to go see what they were so excited about. Why was everything in that hotel white? And what kind of bathroom had a *balcony*? There were also chairs in there, as well as a very odd-looking sink. Modern art. Of course, Sam would appreciate that. The tub wasn't quite big enough to fit an elephant, but you could easily put two or three people in there without having them touch. As soon as I saw the tub, I wanted to fill it with hot water and fall into it. As soon as I unpacked, I planned on taking full advantage before my shift started in a few hours.

Technically, I was already on duty, but I wasn't starting our swing shifts for another hour. That'd give everyone enough time to settle in, and possibly for Ronan to get out of whatever funk he'd slipped into. Maybe he was still mad about our argument on the plane.

After Sam gave me a tour of the bathroom, complete with a demonstration of how the tub worked, I went back to the bedroom to start unpacking. A knock at the suite door interrupted me.

Sam looked up from their phone. "Want me to get it?"

"Nah, I've got it." I tossed the pair of socks in my hands into the top drawer and went out to the main part of the suite.

Ronan stepped out of his bedroom and closed the door behind him, pausing when he saw me. He knew better than to answer the door when I was around. Anyone could be on the other side of that door, including another hitman with a gun. Rather than head for the door, he leaned against the wall and crossed his arms, still sulking.

I ignored the looks he gave me and peered through the peephole. Kai was on the other side. Ronan had said the summer knight was dangerous, and I didn't doubt him for a second, but I didn't think Kai had come up a floor to kill anyone, so I opened the door. Of course, it wasn't until after I opened the door that I realized Mark was standing there with him.

"Kai," I said with a smile. "I figured everyone would still be settling in." I gestured for Mark to go into the suite. Whatever he wanted, we could talk it over after.

He slid past me and hovered at my back, just a little too close for comfort.

"I am," Kai said, shifting his attention from Mark at my back to me. "I just wanted to catch you before you made plans. I know Paris can be overwhelming, especially the first time. I thought I would invite you to dinner. Maybe I can show you a few spots of interest?"

I blinked. That was unexpected. No one invited me to dinner. Well, except for Ronan and he didn't count, did he? "I… Well, I'd love to, but I'm about to start my shift."

"Oh, I can take that for you," Mark said.

I could've smacked him. It wasn't that I didn't want to go out with Kai, but I didn't want to go the first night we were in Paris, especially with Ronan mad at me. I could practically feel my boss's eyes burning holes in the back of my head. If I accepted, he'd be even more upset. Not that I expected he'd do anything about it, especially after the fuss he'd made on the plane about having a personal life.

I shifted my weight, leaning against the doorway with

one hand. "Actually, yeah. I'd love to go out to dinner with you."

Kai's smile brightened. "Perfect. I'll meet you in the lobby at seven-thirty."

"See you then." I closed the door.

Ronan hadn't moved from his spot next to the bedroom door, although he looked even more upset than before, as expected. He said nothing but just stood there, looking miserable.

"It's not a date," I pointed out. "I'm only going to find out more about the summer court, something you've encouraged me to do."

He stood straighter and looked at Mark for support. "I didn't say anything, did I?"

"No, sir," Mark stammered.

"Callie is free to spend her time with whoever she wants," Ronan said, finally stepping out of the corner. He put his hand on the bedroom door. "And so am I."

I expected him to slam the door like an angry teenager when he disappeared behind it, but it closed with a calm click of the lock. Somehow, that was even more irritating. He should've shouted at me, or at least shown he was upset. I would've known how to deal with that. This new, more reserved, and calm Ronan was strangely unsettling. I didn't like him this way.

Well, good thing I don't have to spend the evening with him, I thought and turned to Mark, crossing my arms. "What did you need, Mark?"

He twisted his fingers around a stray thread on his shirt. "I was just wondering if we'd have a translator available. My French is a bit rusty, and the other two only seem to know a little. If there's an emergency, we'll need someone who can speak fluent French."

"Ronan speaks fluent French," I told him.

"Yes, but if something were to happen to him?"

I put a hand on Mark's shoulder. "Mark, almost everyone here speaks very good English. If there's a problem, I'm sure we can find someone to help. We're only going to be here for a few days. If you're concerned about it, why don't you brush up? Guarding Ronan tonight is going to be pretty low key. After the trip, I'm sure all he wants to do is take a nap. There won't be any official events until tomorrow. You're going to be okay, okay?"

He nodded emphatically. "Yes, ma'am."

"Callie," I corrected.

Mark smiled and nodded again. "Right. Callie."

"Good. Now, if you don't mind, I've got a date with a garden tub." I patted him on the shoulder and went back to the bedroom to tell Sam.

CHAPTER FIVE

Kai and I went to one of the restaurants in the hotel, Epicure. A sign outside boasted the chef had earned a prestigious award and I believed it, based on the ambiance alone. Epicure was the sort of place I only expected to see in movies. White tablecloths practically glowed under warm lights. Floral curtains had been drawn over the windows, making the space seem smaller and more intimate. Like everywhere else in the hotel, the tables each had a vase stuffed with deep red roses. The chairs were comfortable enough that I could've slept in them.

The waiters in their formal suits served us water in wine glasses and brought us a separate menu just for the wine. I flipped through it, pretending I knew what I was looking for. The truth was, I barely understood the regular menu, let alone the wine menu. Nothing had prices next to it either. Epicure wasn't the sort of place you went to eat if you cared how much your dinner cost.

It wasn't packed, but every table had at least one person. Business must've been good, and it was easy to see why, judging by the dishes that were being brought out. The portions might've been tiny, but no one seemed disappointed by the food. This was Paris, after all, one of the world's premier locations for fine dining.

"Do you have a favorite?" Kai asked.

"Huh?" I lowered the menu to find him staring at me, an amused smile on his lips. "Oh, you mean the wine." I set the menu aside. "No, not really. To be honest, I'm not much of a wine girl. I've always just had beer or a Coke."

"I'm not much of a drinker, but we are in Paris, and I've been told it's not French cuisine unless you have wine." Kai picked up the wine menu and handed it to the waiter when he returned. "Whatever you recommend would be fine."

The waiter nodded and hurried off to fill the order.

"This place seems kind of exclusive," I said, glancing around. I'd dressed up, even putting on heels for the occasion, but I still felt underdressed compared to most of the women in the restaurant. I spied Natalie at a corner table with three others. One of them was Vaughn. For all I knew, they were all vampires.

"It's usually a three-month wait to get reservations, or so I'm told." Kai picked up his water and took a sip before placing it back on the table. "When Natalie and the vampire aristocracy rented out the whole hotel, however, they included the restaurants and the spa."

"Probably safer that way. Wouldn't want the vamps tempted by unsuspecting humans wandering in and out."

He followed my gaze and frowned. "Not a fan of vampires?"

I eyed him. "Are you?"

Kai shrugged. "I think there's plenty of hate and distrust

to go around. No reason for me to add to it. They haven't done anything to me personally, but I understand why most of our people don't trust them. I heard about your adventure with Jax last month. One of my people was telling me all about it earlier tonight. Apparently, I'm having dinner with a hero." He picked up his glass again and raised it to me.

I smiled and shook my head. "I'm not a hero. I was just doing my job."

"You must be good at it. Ronan only hires the best."

I huffed out a quick laugh. "Maybe someone should remind him of that."

"He doesn't appreciate the work you've done?" Kai placed his glass back on the table but kept his fingers twined around the narrow stem.

It was my turn to shrug. "I think he does. I also think he takes a lot of unnecessary risks. We have different ideas about what constitutes personal security."

"Life's not safe. Even if you close every loophole, if someone wanted to hurt him, they'd find a way. That's one reason I don't bother with security. I don't see the point."

"You're also the summer knight, which seems to make people think twice about challenging you. You wouldn't be where you are if you didn't have a handle on how to protect yourself."

"True," he agreed, spinning the glass. "I know I shouldn't ask, but do you have any thoughts about which court you'll give your allegiance to?"

"Not yet. I'd like to know more about the summer court before I go making any decisions."

Kai sprouted another smile. "I'm happy to answer any

questions you might have. Of course, it won't be a proper substitute for going there yourself. You're welcome anytime."

I considered my first question carefully. One of the reasons I was hesitant to join the winter court was because I'd met Mab. Most fae had a flare for the dramatic, as evidenced by Ronan's mild temper tantrum earlier, but Mab took the cake. I hated how she wielded her power, always flaunting it, using it to manipulate Ronan and everyone she met. She treated me as if I were an object to be won, caring only about what power I might bring to her side. I needed to know if Titania was the same, but I couldn't ask her knight if she was power-hungry.

I put my elbow on the table and leaned my chin on my palm. "Tell me about Titania. What's she like? What's it like working for her?"

"Let's see." Kai turned his eyes to the ceiling in thought. "It's a job, to put it lightly. I don't hate it. I don't love it. I'm not married to my work like the winter knight is. I like my free time and my independence, and Titania is usually inclined to let me have what I want, provided it's within reason."

"She still made you come to this." I gestured around.

"The peace celebration?" He laughed. "Oh, no. I volunteered."

"I don't understand. Why would you want to come here?"

"If I didn't, Titania would be here in my place, and I'd have to come anyway to keep her safe. It's better for everyone that I came here on my own. Besides, I like to travel. As nice as Hawaii is this time of year, I've always wanted to see the world. You? Why are you here?"

"Aside from guarding Ronan, you mean?" I sat up. "Well, we were supposed to go to Spain, but Mab had other ideas. She decided we were coming."

Kai frowned. "Didn't even give you the option?"

"Nope. She just showed up and told us we were going."

"Titania wouldn't do that." Kai shook his head. "She takes a direct interest in her court affairs, though between you and me," he leaned in and put a hand beside his mouth as he whispered, "I don't think the vampires wanted the queens here."

"Why's that?"

"How would they house that much ego under one roof?" He smiled, and we shared a pleasant laugh. "In all seriousness, I don't mind the work. As far as Titania goes, she's like Mab in a way. She's old and powerful. One can only spend so much time at the top of the food chain before you get bored and start trouble."

"Are you saying Titania would favor a war?"

He shrugged. "I'm saying she and Mab are both itching for something big to occupy their time. If they don't fight the vampires, they'll fight each other. They're warrior queens, Callie. It's what they do. This peace celebration marks the longest everyone has been at peace in recorded history. Something is bound to go wrong, and soon. I can feel it in the air. Can't you?"

I glanced over where Vaughn sat with his back to me. Kai didn't know just how right he was.

The waiter came with a bottle of wine and filled our glasses. He inquired about our order, but we'd been so busy talking that neither of us had looked at the menu. We flipped through the small menu while the waiter wandered off to check on another table. It included langoustine, duck foie gras, and pigeon, none of which I'd ever had. There wasn't a steak to be seen, or I would've gravitated toward that.

"You know what I could really go for?" Kai said and flipped the menu closed.

"What's that?"

"A pizza."

I closed my menu and set it aside. "I didn't see that on the menu."

"That's because it's not on the menu." He grinned and dropped his menu to the table. "What do you say I pay for this bottle of wine, and we go find a nice bar where they sell greasy pizza and beer?"

I smiled back. "I'd say that's the best idea you've had all night."

We left Epicure behind after settling the bill and leaving a nice tip, braving the crowded evening streets of Paris. There were a few bars on the same street as the hotel, but all of them seemed to attract an upscale clientele. To get a proper pizza and a good beer, we had to take a car to a less affluent neighborhood nearby.

The pub we wound up in was packed with locals huddled in the glow coming off the lights on the walls. There were no televisions anywhere, and just a touch of neon behind the bar for ambiance. Intimate booths lined the walls, while tables dotted the floor and locals propped up the counter, chatting with the bartender.

We slid into one of the booths and put in our order. I

ordered a personal pizza, no sauce and extra cheese and a pint of locally brewed beer. To my surprise, Kai asked for the same.

I blinked. "You ordered your pizza without sauce. You're not just doing that to copy me because you think it'll win you points, are you?"

"No, not at all." He handed the waitress our menus. "I don't mind tomatoes, but there's something about the texture of tomato sauce on bread. It's—"

"Slimy," I finished.

"Exactly. I don't mind it on spaghetti or in any other pasta dish, but it makes the bread soggy, and the cheese gets that weird texture."

I nodded emphatically. "I've never met anyone who ordered their pizza that way except for me."

Kai smiled. "There's a first time for everything, isn't there?"

Unlike at Epicure, I actually felt overdressed for the pub and kept drawing looks from some of the older men at the bar, or women in jackets and jeans. Or maybe they were looking at Kai. He'd come in wearing a three-piece suit, although he'd since pulled off the tie.

"This is much better," he said after our beers had been delivered. "Don't you think?"

I took a sip and immediately agreed. "Ronan's always trying to take me out to fancy places like that. I suppose that's what he's used to, but I don't fit in."

"Why not?"

I shrugged and picked up my pint. "Guess I'm just not used to it. I grew up in the foster care system and went straight into the Army. Comfort is almost a foreign concept."

"That's a shame. I'm sorry you had to go through that, Callie." He reached across the table, putting his hand over mine. "That must've been hard, growing up like that. I wouldn't wish it on anyone."

"Wasn't so bad." I chugged half the pint and put it down, wiping my mouth clean. "Wow, sorry. I must look like I've got no manners."

"We're in a pub. I don't think manners are a requirement."

"Maybe." I pulled my hand away, eager to change the conversation away from my past and get back to the reason I'd agreed to go out with him. "So, tell me more about the summer court. Give me your best sales pitch. Why should I join your side over Ronan's?"

"See," he said, waving a finger at me, "that's the wrong way to think of this. There are no sides. It's more about fit. Most of us don't get to choose, but for you who do, you need to think carefully about it because you'll be bound for life. So will your children and theirs. You're not just committing to following your queen for a lifetime. It's for eternity."

"Gee, thanks for the pressure."

"I'm not trying to up the pressure on you, Callie. I'm just trying to make sure you understand it's not a decision that should be entered into lightly."

I knew it was an important decision, but I hadn't considered that it might affect future generations, if that ever happened. Now that I was thinking about the future, I realized my decision would ripple through my life and everyone in it. If I chose to join summer, I would lose my job. Without a regular paycheck, Sam and I might lose the loft. Hell, Sam and Ronan had become friends since all this began. I might even lose my best friend in the whole world if I let Mab bully me. Ronan had assured me that no matter what I chose, he'd back my play, but those were just words. When it came down to it, he'd always done whatever his mother said. If she told him to fire me, he'd feel bad about it, but I was growing more certain every day that he'd do it.

On the other hand, if I joined the winter court, I'd be Mab's subject. She'd use me. After seeing what I was capable of, I was sure it wouldn't be for anything good, either. Mab would turn me into some sort of weapon or a threat. I didn't want that any more than I wanted to lose Sam. The whole situation was FUBAR.

"I know how serious the decision is," I said. "I'm taking it seriously. That's why I'm here."

"And I thought it was because of my irresistible charm." Kai smiled and took a drink. "When you get right down to it, the courts are the same in all the basic ways. There's a queen you'll owe your unwavering loyalty to, court functions you'll probably have to attend, orders you'll have to obey. Most of the differences boil down to the details. Winter is cold, their egos brittle, their social interactions distant. They're winter. I find Summer is warmer in more than just ambient temperature. The people smile more. They're more open. We have beach parties. They have formal balls. Winter is elegant and rigid. We're fun and flexible."

I wanted to doubt what he was telling me, but he sounded sincere. Not only that, but I'd been to the winter court. I'd met the winter knight and seen the palace of ice. I couldn't fathom Mab having a beach party, but it was easy to imagine Kai laughing and having a beer on a beach. He'd seem right at home there.

Our pizzas came. Half the time, when I ordered mine without sauce, I had to send it back because they'd put sauce on it, thinking that was a mistake, or misunderstanding my order. Not this time. The French pub's pizza was arguably the best I'd had in my life.

"So, any more questions about the summer court?" Kai asked after we'd both devoured half our respective personal pizzas.

I ran a napkin over my fingers and set it aside. "Not about the summer court, but maybe you can help me understand something about the winter court. Why is the winter knight so...weird?"

"You mean, the mask and the silence." Kai gestured to his face.

I nodded.

"How can I put this?" He sighed and glanced upward. "It's not my place to explain that. Maybe that's a question better left for Ronan to answer?"

"I've asked him. He just says I shouldn't worry about it."

"Then maybe he's right." Kai smiled and dug back into his pizza.

We didn't talk about the courts the rest of the evening, but we did talk late into the night. We stayed in the pub past midnight, until all the regular patrons had left. About the time the bartender started wiping down tables and putting up chairs, we decided we should get out of there.

While I'd had a few pints, neither of us had drunk

enough to call ourselves inebriated, although I thought he was a little more on the tipsy side than me. He had said he wasn't much of a drinker. Rather than get in a car and go straight back to Le Bristol, we decided to take a stroll and see if he could walk it off. The last thing he wanted was to trip into his suite half-drunk and have a call waiting from the queen.

"Does she call you often?" I asked as we walked down the street.

"Often enough. I'm her knight. Of course, she does. And I'm here, doing important...stuff." He gestured vaguely at nothing.

"This peace summit is important?"

"Not really. It's more of a show for important people to see and be seen. Bullshit court politics on both sides, I think."

We came across a street vendor who was closing up for the night. I convinced him in broken French to sell us a few bottles of water. They were grossly overpriced, but I paid what he wanted and handed a bottle to Kai. "Drink the whole thing before you go to bed, or you'll regret it tomorrow."

"D'you do this often? Go wandering around pubs with strange men you barely know?"

I laughed. "Hell, no. I don't even go out with my room-mate most of the time. I suppose Ronan's right about one thing. I'm bad at having fun."

"Well," said Kai, drawing up to a stop in front of the hotel's side entrance, "you should join the summer court. You'll learn to have fun there. It's practically a mandate. Consider this a formal invitation." He tore the cap off and swallowed a mouthful of water. "I think we should part ways here. I'm glad we had this evening, Callie."

"Me too."

He picked up my hand and kissed it as he had in the car on the way over before turning and going up the steps, only stumbling a little.

I restrained a laugh and called after him, "Drink the water!"

Rather than go in the side entrance, I went around front, feeling elated. I wasn't going to call the outing a date, but if it was, it would've been one of the best I'd ever been on. Kai and I had connected on some level. It was like we understood each other. We were already finishing each other's sentences. He was smart, charming, easy on the eyes… Maybe I should join the summer court. I felt like I'd get along with him a lot better than I did Ronan.

I came through the front door and paused a few steps into the lobby as I spied Mark standing near the elevators. Alone. No Ronan in sight. I glanced at my phone, checking the time. He was supposed to be on shift for another thirty minutes. What was he doing down in the lobby?

"Hi, Mark," I said, approaching. "Where's Ronan? Why aren't you with him?"

He jumped at the sound of my voice. "Callie! Wow, you look great! I mean…"

I put a hand on his shoulder. "Where is Ronan?"

Mark gestured to the elevator. "Upstairs. He told me to get lost for a while, so I came down here. He told Yvonne to go to bed."

I barely waited for him to finish speaking before I ran for the stairs. If I waited for the elevator, it might be too late. It was one thing to leave Ronan alone in his room, but I'd explicitly told everyone that the suite was to remain guarded. No one was supposed to come and go without being logged. Why would Ronan send his protection away? To get back at me for going out with Kai? That idiot!

I raced up the stairs two at a time and burst onto the fourth-floor hallway, fumbling to get out the room key. As I suspected, Yvonne had obeyed Ronan. There was no one guarding him.

The door popped open and I pushed through it, flipping on the lights. The main room was empty, but someone had been there. There was a broken glass on the floor, the largest piece stained with blood.

There was a muffled sound in Ronan's bedroom. I grabbed a gun from the case near the front door and went to Ronan's door. It was locked, but one good kick had it open. Two shadows wrestled in the dim light. "Freeze!"

A female voice shrieked something in French.

Wait, a woman? I flipped on the light.

There was a naked woman in Ronan's bed, scrambling to pull the sheet up to her chin.

He was half-undressed. "For God's sake, Callie! Knock next time!"

It wasn't until he shouted at me that I realized I hadn't barged in on a threat, I'd interrupted one of his hookups.

CHAPTER SIX

I went back out to the living room area and sat on the sofa with my arms crossed while Ronan and his guest got dressed. Apparently, my interruption had killed the mood. I didn't care. Inside, I was still steaming because he'd brought someone into the suite after we'd explicitly discussed why he shouldn't do that. What was he thinking?

Maybe I should quit. Ronan doesn't listen to me anyway. I don't think he even appreciates all the work I do to keep his stupid ass safe. In one move, he'd thrown away hours of planning. What if one of the vampires had decided to bust in instead of me? I'd be mopping up bloodstains, that's what.

The bedroom door opened. I pretended not to be paying attention as Ronan tried to reassure the stranger.

"You don't have to go," he said, probably for the hundredth time.

"I think I had better." The woman had a thick French accent but spoke in English. Was that for my benefit or his?

"It is getting late, and they'll be wondering where I am. There's always tomorrow."

"Can I call you?"

"Yes, please." She kissed him briefly on the cheek and grinned before turning and waving to me. "Bye-bye, now."

Gag me with a spoon, I thought. *What a ditz.*

Ronan walked her to the door and held it while she went through it. The room was silent as he shut it behind her and put his back to it, mimicking my pose with crossed arms. We both knew where this conversation was going. Question was, who was going to yell at who first?

"Should I even say it?" I uncrossed my arms and stood so I wouldn't have to argue sitting down.

"Say what?"

"That you should've told Mark and Yvonne what you were doing and had them wait outside the suite door? That you should've cleared her with me first?"

"I don't need you to do a background check on everyone I meet, Callie!" Ronan stormed away from the door and went to the table, where a bottle of wine waited next to an empty glass. He filled the glass halfway. "There's being protective, and there's being overprotective. You've crossed the line, Callie."

"Crossed the line?" I clenched my fists. "A month ago, I saved your life from an assassin three times. An assassin, I might add, who you hired to be your personal trainer."

"How was I supposed to know who he really was?" He shrugged and sipped from the glass.

"That's what a background check is for!" How could he not see it? He'd almost gotten himself killed. Had he learned nothing from the experience?

Ronan leaned against the table. "Tell me, did you do a background check on Kai before you went out with him? Maybe you'd like to hear what I know about him that you don't?"

I rolled my eyes. "I didn't go out with him. It wasn't a date. I told you."

"Yes, you were just going to find out more about the summer court, which is why you put all that on." He gestured at me vaguely.

I looked down at the black dress I'd chosen. "What's wrong with this?"

"Nothing. Nothing at all. That's just not the sort of thing a woman wears to a not-a-date." He slurred his words slightly. Maybe he'd been doing that through the whole conversation, and I'd just missed it because of how pissed off I was.

I marched across the room and pulled the glass away from him before picking up the bottle. It was only a quarter full. "Are you drunk?"

"Maybe." He jerked the bottle away from me, followed by the glass. "You going to yell at me for that too? Is there anything you *don't* want to yell at me for? Especially after you ruined the one thing I was looking forward to?"

I sighed and pinched the bridge of my nose. "Okay, that was an accident. I don't agree with you about the whole personal security thing when it comes to flings, but I wouldn't have barged in on you if I hadn't thought you weren't in danger."

"I was perfectly fine." He wandered over and plopped into a chair.

"What about the broken wine glass? There was blood on it."

"What broken… Oh, this?" He leaned over and picked up the broken wine glass by the stem. "A little foreplay gone wrong. I dropped it and cut my hand picking it up. See?" He showed me his other hand as proof. "It's already healed, as you can see. No danger there. In fact, one could argue you're the most dangerous thing to ever happen to me."

"How's that?" I crossed my arms again. This should be good.

"Well," he said, filling his cup again, "if I hadn't run into you at the factory photoshoot…" He took a sip.

I waited for him to pick the line back up, but he seemed to forget what he was going to say mid-sentence, preferring instead to watch the dark liquid swirl around in his cup. With another sigh, I went to take the glass away from him. This time, he didn't fight me on it.

"Come on, you big, dumb idiot," I said, pulling him to his feet.

"You know, I shouldn't let you talk to me that way. It's insubordination."

I snorted and walked him back to the bedroom. "Go on then. Fire me."

"I couldn't do that. I think I like you too much. Against my better judgment. You're a vicious cycle, Callie Hart. I hate how much I need you."

I hesitated in the middle of pulling open his door. He'd ground the last two lines out like a curse, but the words didn't sound nearly as angry as his tone. "I can go anytime you want," I said, my tone gentle. "If you want me gone, just say the word, and I'll go sign up with the summer court. I'm sure they'll help me find work. Some rich brat there probably needs protecting."

"I don't want you to go," he mumbled. "But I shouldn't say that, should I? It's your decision. I can't get in the way."

"You're allowed to have an opinion." *I want you to have an opinion.* But I couldn't say that out loud, because it would seem too much like I needed him too.

Ronan pushed away from me to stand on his own. "I think maybe I should be sober before we talk again. I'm saying things I shouldn't. If this keeps going, I might say something I can't take back."

I made sure he got into bed before I went around to check the windows and behind the shower curtain, just in case. He was already snoring by the time I finished, so I shut the door as quietly as I could, locking it on my way out.

After I got back from the team suite, where we very thoroughly went over our procedures for times like the one that had just happened, I woke Sam.

"Can you believe him?" I yanked the clip out of my hair and ran my hands through it. "I was gone for what, a few hours? And somehow in that time, he manages to meet a woman, drink too much, cut his hand, and convince her to go back to his hotel room with him. Am I wrong in thinking maybe she was a little too easy? I mean, a woman like that... He's going to catch something, Sam. And I am SO not looking forward to that conversation."

"Uh-huh." Sam yawned and hugged their stuffed owl closer. "Why would he talk to you about it?"

"He talks to me about everything. I know more than I ever wanted to know about his personal life." I tore the cap off a tiny bottle of water and swallowed a mouthful.

Sam rubbed sleep from their eyes with a fist. They'd been out cold when I came in, and I probably should've just let them stay that way, but they were the one who'd asked me how it went with Kai. I still hadn't gotten around to explaining that. We were stuck on Ronan and how stupid he'd been.

"Did you even see her, Sam? And she said 'Bye-bye, now' when she left. Who does that? I bet she's had plastic surgery. Definitely fake boobage."

"Why do you even care?" Sam swung their feet over the side of the couch and planted them firmly on the carpet. "You seem awfully upset that he was about to bang some woman. You sure you're not jealous?"

"Jealous?" I spun around in the chair in front of the vanity and threw my head back to laugh. "Me? Are you serious? Come on, Sam. Ronan's not my type."

"But Kai is?"

"I'm going to tell you the same thing I told Ronan. It was not a date!" I turned back around and started brushing my hair. "Can't a girl go to dinner with a guy without it turning into some romantic rendezvous?"

Sam wasn't totally wrong, though. Given the chance, I might've dated Kai or someone like him, even if I didn't think he was my type. I wasn't the sort to fall head over heels for someone, but I couldn't deny there was something there. It didn't feel like a romantic attraction to me, though, or at least not like any I'd ever felt before.

"He's just easy to talk to," I said out loud. "Kai, not Ronan. I haven't even known him a full twenty-four hours yet, and we're already finishing each other's sentences. I feel like I've known him forever, Sam."

"That settles it." Sam fell to the floor on their back, wiggling the stuffed owl in the air. "Callie and Kai, sitting in a tree—"

"Don't tease me, Sam."

"K-I-S-S-I-N-G!"

"We didn't!" I got up out of the chair and playfully pulled the owl away from them. "But it would be fair to say he's definitely swaying my opinion of the summer court toward the positive side." I dropped the owl on Sam's face. "Ronan's behavior isn't helping. It's like he wants me to join the other side."

"Are there really sides?" Sam hugged their owl. "I mean, both courts are fae, right? So why are they fighting like this? Shouldn't they get along?"

"I don't know." I flopped onto the bed, staring at the ceiling. "There's some sort of tension between them I can't figure out. I need to learn more about the history, but Ronan's never interested in telling me that. Maybe I should ask Kai."

"You're putting an awful lot of faith in that guy." Sam sat up and frowned. "You said so yourself. You barely know him. How do you know if he's going to tell you the truth or some censored version of things?"

I rolled over onto my stomach and propped my head up on a hand. "That's the problem with getting information from both sides. Whatever tensions there are between summer and winter, they downplay it. That shouldn't even be important right now. Kai says to think about it less like choosing a side and more like finding a good fit. You met Mab, Sam. Do you think I'm more like Mab or Kai?"

Ronan had accused me of being cold, and maybe he was right. Somewhere deep down, I knew I was overstepping by putting such harsh restrictions on who came and went. The harder I pushed for him to be safe, the more he'd fight back. Ronan was as bullheaded as a teenager sometimes, but I wasn't his mother. While it was my job to keep him safe, it wasn't right for me to try to lay down the law as I had. It had to be his decision to follow my guidelines or not. And if he didn't, he had to be willing to live—or die— with the consequences. That was what I was worried he didn't understand. Here we were in a strange city, surrounded by enemies and unknowns. Now was the time to be more vigilant than ever, not to relax restrictions.

If I squinted hard, I could also see things from his perspective. I didn't approve of random hookups, but that wasn't my job. I'd sounded like his mother, which was not a comforting thought.

I wanted Sam to say I was more like Kai—warm, gentle, and fun-loving—but that wasn't true, was it? Ronan was right. I was a workaholic who didn't let herself relax and have fun. Maybe joining the summer court would change that.

Sam cringed. "Do you remember that story about how Aphrodite, Hera, and Athena went to Paris to choose the most beautiful one? This is kinda like that. No matter what I answer, it's going to get me in trouble, isn't it?"

I moaned and flopped onto my back. "I'm such an awful person. Maybe I should apologize to Ronan? Except he was a jerk too."

"Do you really think he didn't want you to find out about Olivia?"

"Olivia?" I lifted my head. "Is that her name?"

"Oops. Er, I mean... My point is, maybe the whole reason he brought her in here was for you to find. I mean, it's possible."

I sat up, frowning. "What are you getting at, Sam?"

They shrugged. "Just that maybe he's trying to make *you* jealous?"

"So, first you accuse me of trying to make him jealous, and then vice versa? What do you think this is, Sam, a soap opera?" I snorted and turned to the window. "Besides, I don't care who he sleeps with."

"Then why were you bad-mouthing Olivia so harshly?"

I narrowed my eyes at them. Was it so hard for them to believe I didn't think Olivia—if that really was her name—was good enough for Ronan? Come on! He was a prince. He could have anyone he wanted. Why was he settling for some French bimbo with a boob job? That didn't mean he had to be with me. I couldn't stand the man, and yet...

No. I shook my head. There was a world of difference between Ronan and Kai. Kai understood he didn't have to impress me, and he didn't fight with me over every little thing. Honestly, it was a wonder Ronan hadn't fired me yet, with as many arguments as we'd had lately.

I hate how much I need you. I don't want you to go. The sentences echoed through my mind like they meant something. They didn't. They were just the ramblings of an idiot

drunk who didn't know the first thing about actual relationships.

I grabbed one of the pillows from the head of the bed and flung it at Sam, missing by a mile.

Sam stuck out their tongue. "Missed me!"

"Just shut up and go to sleep."

"Night, Callie."

"Night, Sam."

But it wasn't a good night. I tossed and turned, unable to get those lines out of my head. What if he'd meant them? What, if anything, would that change?

Nothing, because there could never be anything between Ronan and me. He was my boss. I worked for him. That was it. I turned over in bed with a little grunt to stare at the clock. Three fifteen in the morning. Just a few more hours until the alarm went off. With a little luck, I could still get two hours of sleep. Too bad I'd never had much luck to begin with.

CHAPTER SEVEN

The peace celebration began in earnest on the second day, so I aimed to get up before the sun to get through an early shift. I didn't want to be hanging around Ronan in the evening in case he went out with another date.

When I slapped my alarm off and sat up yawning. However, I found I wasn't the first one awake. Sam's loveseat was empty, their blanket neatly folded and the pillow tucked into the corner like it belonged there. I checked the time again. Sam had never been an early riser. Then again, we'd jumped several time zones on our trip to Paris. Maybe that was why they were up.

I hit the bathroom for a quick shower and stepped out of the bedroom minutes later, dressed and ready to gulp down coffee and breakfast before we started on the daily itinerary. When I heard Ronan say my name, I paused out of sight to listen.

"She's made this trip more miserable than my mother ever could have," Ronan said.

That stung. I knew how much he hated his mother. I wasn't *really* worse than her, was I?

"I warned you," Sam replied. "Callie can be overprotective, especially of the people she cares about most."

"I hardly think I register in her top ten. I'm just a job to her."

"I wouldn't be so sure." Sam drew out the pronoun.

"What do you mean?" Ronan asked.

"I mean, I think the reason she was so upset last night has nothing to do with you not listening to her and everything to do with her being jealous."

"Jealous?" Ronan laughed. "Of Olivia?"

"Of anyone you hook up with, Ronan. Callie wants to jump your bones bad."

His dismissive laughter exploded into a full-fledged guffaw that lasted a few minutes and left me fighting to keep from revealing myself. "Oh, that's a good one."

"You telling me you wouldn't?"

"Callie's made it clear she's not interested. I asked her out, and she shut me down, remember?"

I wracked my brain, trying to recall a specific moment where he'd asked me on a date and I'd declined but coming up empty.

Something hissed. It sounded like he'd dropped liquid on the coffee burner and smelled like it too. "Callie's right about one thing, though. Olivia's just a warm body. But that's the life I live. She doesn't get to gripe at me for having company after she refused the offer. And would it kill her to relax a little bit?"

"I keep telling her she needs to get laid. She'd feel better."

"As long as it's not with Kai."

I decided that was as good a time as any to interrupt and came around the corner to find the two of them at the dining room table. They'd moved the coffee maker there and plugged it in to enjoy two cups of awful watered-down coffee, which was how Ronan always made it.

"Callie!" Sam grinned and raised their paper cup. "We were just talking about you!"

I pulled the coffee pot off the burner and frowned at the light brown bean-water. "You guys know we're in Paris, right? And this hotel has room service and fancy restaurants downstairs? You could have gourmet coffee delivered."

"I've ordered some," Ronan said and rubbed his forehead. "I just didn't want to wait. I've got a splitting headache."

"Wine hangovers are the worst," Sam agreed.

Knowing that decent coffee was coming, I decided I could be patient. I sank into the third chair at the table. Rather than speak to or acknowledge Ronan, I turned to Sam. "Sam, could you let Ronan know I've adjusted his security schedule for the day? I'll be handing my shifts off to the others so I can enjoy the city."

They took a deep breath and looked at Ronan.

"I can hear her just fine, Sam." Ronan sighed and placed his coffee on the table. "Don't be a child, Callie."

I ignored him. I was a grown woman. I got to be petty if I wanted.

"At least tell me where you're going in case I need to reach you," Ronan said.

"Sam, you can tell Ronan he can reach me by phone like

he would any other employee on their day off. As for where I'm going, I don't know yet. That depends on what Kai wants to do. Maybe I'll go spend the day with him." I said it deliberately to get under his skin, expecting him to get angry, to explode.

Instead, he sank into that chilling calm. "Callie, there's something you need to know about Kai before you get more involved with him."

There was a knock at the door, and a small voice on the other side announced they were from room service. I jumped out of my chair, relieved by the timely interruption and excited by the idea of coffee. The coffee Ronan had ordered turned out to be these tiny teacups of espresso, two ounces at most. I downed mine at the door and handed it back to the bellhop, along with the order to bill the room. I returned to the table with the other two cups and their saucers, placing them in the middle of the table so I wouldn't have to interact with Ronan.

Ronan didn't even reach for the coffee. "Callie, like I said—"

"I don't want to hear it, Ronan," I snapped. "You've already said enough on the topic. You told me he was dangerous, to be careful, to watch out for him."

"That's not what—"

"Well, whatever it is, it'll have to wait." I stood and pocketed my phone. "If we don't leave right now, we're going to miss the opening ceremonies, and your mother did say you had to be seen. Go on. Drink your coffee, and let's go."

Ronan pushed it away.

Sam eagerly downed theirs and Ronan's before rising

and declaring, "Have fun, you two. I've got an art gallery tour this morning. We'll catch up this evening, right?"

"Right." I hugged Sam.

They practically ran out of the suite, leaving me alone with Ronan.

I didn't give him time to pick up the conversation where he left off, going straight to the door and holding it open for him. "Better hurry."

He gave me a long look as if he wanted to continue, then stood, adjusted his jacket, and marched out ahead of me.

The ballroom was already crowded. Vampires and fae milled around, holding glasses full of orange juice or what I hoped was wine. Never could tell with vampires. Everyone was dressed in semiformal attire except for me. I'd put on comfortable shoes, a loose-fitting pair of black pants, and a nice button-up white shirt. It made me stick out like a sore thumb among the suits with ties and fancy cocktail dresses. Apparently their security people had gotten a memo I hadn't.

The ballroom was a large, beautiful space. The floor was polished marble. Above us, skylights let in the late morning sun. Glittering silver chandeliers curved like reverse jellyfish toward the ceiling. Ivory columns spun from floor to ceiling, the only thing breaking up the party. On the far side of the room were buffet tables offering up every sort of brunch food imaginable, from a wide array of tarts and muffins to miniature omelets made to order.

Normally, I might've followed Ronan around the room, just so I could be there in case something happened. However, after last night, I decided it was best to give him his space. While Ronan wandered around the room, shaking hands, and making polite small talk with people I didn't know, I took up a post near the buffet table and snagged a muffin. I hadn't been hungry until we walked into the room, and the smell of food reminded me that I had skipped breakfast in favor of coffee. There was more coffee on another table, but I went for the orange juice.

No one talked to me. I was the hired help, which my clothing probably made obvious. I was no one of interest to any of them. As far as they were concerned, I was just another member of the hotel staff, which I was just fine with. The fancy brunch party was not my scene, and unlike Ronan, I didn't have to be seen.

I did spend a little time scanning the crowd for Kai, but I came up empty at first. It wasn't until we had been at the party for twenty minutes that he ambled in. Like Ronan, he shook hands with several people and wandered around the room making small talk. I guess that sort of thing was expected of the court delegates. I was just glad I didn't have to do it.

From my spot next to the buffet table, I spied Vaughn's familiar bald head coming through a nearby door. He paused just inside and gave me an acknowledging nod that I ignored. Vaughn Meyer was the last person I wanted to speak to, especially now that I was finally starting to be into a better mood. Which was, of course, why he must have decided to come over.

"Enjoying the party?" he said, picking up an apple tart.

I looked at him blankly. "I'm working. Buzz off."

"Now, there's no need for that. Whatever tensions have been between us in the past, I hope to leave those behind going forward." He put one hand in his suit pocket and took a bite of the tart. "You really can't find pastries like this outside Paris. Please tell me you've at least tried the food."

"I'm not here for the food or the sights. If it were up to me, I wouldn't be here."

Vaughn smiled, showing his fangs. "Are you and Ronan no longer getting along so well, then?"

"If we weren't, it wouldn't be any of your business, now would it?"

Vaughn made a noise that was somewhere between a snort and a grunt. "I suppose not. You might not believe me, but I am glad to see you well."

"You're right. I don't believe you." I crossed my arms and watched Ronan slip gracefully between a vampire and a fae who both reached to shake his hand at once.

"You know, you should keep a tighter leash on your employer." Vaughn picked up a glass and filled it with the dark liquid, which I was beginning to suspect wasn't actually wine. "I'm surprised to see you hanging back. Anything could happen out there on the floor. Vampires and fae mingling together." He uttered the last line with disdain.

"This is supposed to be a peace celebration," I said. "Unlike you, I think the rest of vampire kind prefers peace over war. And there is a lot of security in the room." Which was why I was the only one on-shift today. Natalie had requested that we allow it to look like we trusted her security.

"You are grossly misinformed, Ms. Hart." He sipped from his glass. "My kind thrives on conflict."

I followed Vaughn's eyes, expecting to find him aiming

his gaze of ill intent at one of the fae, or maybe even Ronan. Instead, he watched Natalie as she worked her way through the crowd, smiling, shaking hands, and greeting people. She came up to Ronan and kissed him on either cheek, taking his hand as her smile widened. The expression on Vaughn's face was practically murderous.

"You don't approve of the way Natalie interacts with the fae?" I asked.

Vaughn lowered his glass. "What I approve and disapprove of in my aristocracy is, quite frankly, not your concern. Every court, the vampires included, has internal strife. Each one could use a little improvement somewhere. I'm sure even you can agree on that."

I did, but I wasn't going to tell him that. I was desperate for the encounter to come to an end. Hell, I was ready to leave not just the party, but also Paris, and we'd only been there for a day. "What do you want, Vaughn?"

"Exactly what I've said. That you should be more careful. There are those here who wish Ronan harm."

I turned to Vaughn. "Like you?"

He frowned. "If I meant him harm, he would be dead."

"Big words from a man who failed his first attempt at assassination of a fae prince."

"An anomaly, I assure you. Contract work is always a roll of the dice. I learned my lesson. If you want something done right, you do it yourself. However, I've lost interest in your employer. If I were to make a move, I would set my sights much higher." He smiled at me smugly.

I lowered my voice so the guests nearby wouldn't hear. "Are you saying you're plotting against one of the fae queens?"

"I'm not saying anything. Those are your words, not mine." He took another sip of his drink, then placed it on a passing tray. "I should wish you good luck. You'll need it in the coming days." With an exaggerated bow, Vaughn backed away and disappeared into the crowd.

I tried to find him, just to keep an eye on where he was going and what he was up to, but there was no sign of him anywhere.

Someone struck a glass, calling our attention to the front of the room. Natalie had found her way there and stood on a small stage, glass in hand, all smiles. "Welcome to the annual peace celebration! For those of you who don't know me, my name is Natalie, and it is my honor to host this gala. Today, we gather to commemorate our joint decision to suspend hostilities between our peoples. Since the end of the war, both the fae and the vampires have entered into a period of relative prosperity. There can be no doubt that this lasting peace is a good thing for all of us. Over the last year, we have celebrated many advances in industry on both sides. Our peoples have shown the capacity to do great good when we work together. In short, we are better acting together than we ever were apart. Friends, let us raise our glasses in a toast to one another, to the progress of years, to many years of peace, and more to come."

"To peace!" Dozens of filled glasses surged into the air, joining Natalie in her toast.

I was finally able to spot Vaughn, but only because he was the only one besides me in the room who didn't raise his glass.

CHAPTER EIGHT

Ronan approached me after the toast. I figured he was as done as I was with all the socializing and looking forward to retreating back to the room. Maybe we could order lunch and have a nice, relaxing day. Or maybe I could convince him to go out and we could meet Sam for one of their tours. I wasn't that into art, but staring at paintings and sculptures all day was preferable to spending any more time in that room with those people.

"Are you ready to get out of here?" Ronan asked.

"I thought you'd never ask." I placed my empty glass on the nearby table.

"Excellent, because I have a lunch date I need to get to."

I looked to Ronan, frowning, as we walked toward the exit. "Your schedule for today didn't mention anything about lunch date. I'll have to call one of the other guards to join us."

"Oh, didn't it? I must've forgotten to add it. And we don't have time." He shoved his hands in his pockets. By the smug smile he was trying so hard to hide, I figured he must have forgotten it on purpose.

"Who is your date this time?"

"Someone you want to run a background check on?" Ronan raised an eyebrow and slowed his walk slightly.

I stopped, forcing him to stop with me if he wanted to continue the conversation. "Ronan, your personal life is your business. I'm not going to stop giving you security advice, not even personal security advice. That's my job. It's what you hired me to do. However, I acknowledge that it's up to you to follow it or not. As long as you're willing to live with the consequences of your decisions, you're free to do as you want. I'm not your mother, and you're a grown man who should take responsibility for himself."

I thought the speech would make him happy, settle the tensions between us. Instead, he seemed disappointed. He started walking again, this time slower. "It's a moot point anyway. You've already met her."

"You mean that Olivia girl from last night?" And here I'd thought she was just a fling. Since when did Ronan have lunch dates with a fling? *Maybe this is more than that.*

Ronan nodded. "I thought taking her out would make up for last night. Don't worry, Callie. We'll be back for your shift change. I promise."

I couldn't help but scowl. "We'd better be. I'll have Jim meet us there if you'll tell me where we're going."

***

Ronan brought Olivia to a café whose name was in French. If I'd tried to pronounce it, I was sure I would've tangled the words so badly someone somewhere would've gotten cursed. It was a quaint little place with all the Parisian charm you'd expect. Tiny little tables with pretty tablecloths, decorative vases full of flowers, orchestral music playing in the background somewhere. I suppose you'd even call it romantic if you were into that sort of thing.

I wasn't. I was just bored.

While they enjoyed gourmet French onion soup, some crepes, and split a baguette, Jim and I hovered on the other side of the room. I was on my phone, trying to find out what I could about Olivia. I was glad I'd grabbed the muffin at the opening ceremonies because I wasn't going to get anything to eat during Ronan's lunch date. He wanted us on alert and out of sight, which was fine with me, even if my stomach protested with a growl on occasion.

Unfortunately, he had been right about Olivia. She was squeaky-clean, not even a parking ticket on her record. More than that, she was downright boring. Olivia's day job was playing the flute in a local orchestra. Her father was a wealthy art collector, her mother a fashion designer. Once I found all that out, it became a little clearer why he was so smitten with her. Outside of his modeling job, Ronan's major hobby was music. He'd always wanted to be part of an orchestra or a band. It was something he talked about frequently. Not only that, but he was also a collector of art, and as a model, he had connections in the fashion industry as well.

No wonder they'd gotten together. She was a part of his world in a way I could never be. I had no interest in art, knew nothing about fashion, and couldn't play a musical instrument to save my life. Olivia was everything that I would never be.

Why am I drawing that comparison? I don't want to be anything like her. And it's not like I'm competing for Ronan's affections. I work for him. I do my job. I go home. That's all there is. I glanced up from my phone to see him grinning like an idiot at her. She smiled and batted her eyelashes before he put a buttered slice of the baguette into her mouth. I thought I was going to vomit, they were so cute. It was like being on the set of a bad romantic comedy. Ronan wasn't even acting like himself. Maybe he was under some sort of spell. If only I could dismiss it so easily, but I didn't think that was what was going on. As he'd said, he was lonely, and Olivia provided the type of meaningless company he was looking for.

I wondered for a moment what it would be like to live her life, to have grown up with a family and never have to question where my next meal would come from. What would it be like to always have a roof over my head, to know where I was going to sleep every night? Before I moved in with Sam, the Army was the first place I never had lacked that certainty. I'd spent too much of my childhood bouncing from home to home, learning that it was a waste of time to form lasting relationships. Maybe that was what was wrong with me.

I closed my eyes and clenched my fist around my phone. *There's nothing wrong with me. I'm not that scared little girl anymore.* While I was in the military, the first thing they taught me was that if I was unhappy with my situation, I should do what I could to change it. Maybe I couldn't change broad strokes like being shipped off to war or where I was assigned, but I could change how I reacted to it. I was letting Olivia and Ronan get under my skin because I was too focused on that.

I shook myself. I had to pay attention to work. Ronan and Olivia wrapped up their lunch and stood. I tucked my phone away.

In the rental car, I rode up front, so I didn't have to pretend it didn't bother me that the two of them were making out in the back seat. Jim took a separate car back. From the passenger seat, I focused on scrolling through my social media and waiting for Sam to text me back. Why weren't they replying? They probably had to turn off their phone while they were in a museum or something, I reasoned. Part of me was in panic mode, worried that something happened to Sam, but that was normal. I was always worried about someone.

As soon as we arrived at the hotel, I called Mark to come and take over. My shift didn't technically end for another fifteen minutes, but I didn't want to be around when Ronan took Olivia up to the room. I sure as hell wasn't going to sit in the living area while those two went at it. Mark came down to the lobby and met us at the elevators. Jim joined us at the same time.

I made the exchange, handing over the few personal items Ronan had given me to carry. "Good luck, Mark," I said. "This should be an easy shift for you. Don't let Ronan get rid of you this time. If he sends you away, just park it outside the suite door and wait. You can order room service. Put it on his tab. As we discussed last night, *never* leave him unguarded. Next time, it's your job."

"Yes, ma'am," Mark said, fumbling to juggle his phone

and Ronan's watch. "I promise what happened last night won't happen again."

I waved a hand. "*Callie*, Mark. Call me Callie." Having him call me "ma'am" reminded me too much of my military days, and I didn't want this job to become like that.

I stood outside the elevator on the bottom floor until it reached our floor. After that, Ronan was no longer my responsibility for the rest of the day. I decided rather than go straight for the city tour, I would enjoy a drink first. The hotel had an upscale bar, and I went to find myself a seat there. It was the middle of the day, so it wasn't very crowded, which was just fine with me. I'd had enough of crowds. There were a few faces I recognized from the peace celebration's opening ceremony, important people who must've stepped away for the same reasons I had—too many people in small spaces. We ignored each other amicably.

I ordered a beer and a simple pastry. It was kind of nice to be able to sit alone and not worry about what everyone else was up to.

I should be paying more attention to enjoying myself, I thought. *What am I going to do with myself for the rest of the day?*

I pulled out my phone, opened my contacts, and scrolled through them until I found Kai's name. He'd given me his personal cell number the night before and invited me to call him anytime. If Ronan could go out with Olivia whenever he wanted, I could go out with Kai. I sent him a quick text, asking what he was up to for the rest of the day.

He answered in a matter of minutes, apologizing and saying he had meetings with people for most of the rest of the afternoon, but he was available that evening if I wanted to go to dinner. I shot back a tentative yes and immediately scrolled to Sam's number. I sent them a text too, asking what their plans were. While I waited for them to respond, I went searching for local events, trying to narrow down things I might be interested in if they were too busy to hang out. There was a wine and cheese tasting at a nearby restaurant, but I'd never been a fan of wine. Maybe it would change my mind. A little theater on the other side of town was having a show, but I couldn't read the title since it was a jumble of French. Could be good for a surprise. Even if I didn't speak the language, I could appreciate the acting and the costumes.

Maybe I should just take a tour of the city, I thought. There was an open-air bus tour, but I didn't want to get grouped in with the rest of the tourists. I needed to choose something I could walk away from quickly if I needed to. I stared at the screen. Why bother? I had to start trusting the other bodyguards eventually. Ronan had hired them to do their jobs because I thought they were capable. Here I was, looking for something to fill my time and to enjoy myself, and I was still thinking about work. Not this time.

My phone buzzed. I picked it up and turned it over to find Sam had finally texted me back. They were in the middle of a multi-museum tour that didn't end for another two hours. I was on my own until then. Easy enough. I could fill two hours alone in Paris.

I glanced around the bar, pausing when I spied a security camera tucked into a corner. That reminded me I still needed to get with Natalie and the hotel management to coordinate security for the next day. I would find her as soon as I ate.

Vaughn appeared next to me as my food arrived.

I rolled my eyes. "Go away, Vaughn. I'm not in the mood, and I'm off-duty."

He grabbed me by the arm and hauled me from my seat.

I jerked my arm away after a few steps. "What the hell? You can't just drag me away from the bar!"

Vaughn leaned in close and spoke through his teeth. "I'm not here speaking to you for my health. I'm here to warn you. My intelligence has informed me that Ronan might be in danger."

I stared at the vampire for a moment and then pretended to dust off my jacket. "Why would you be telling me that?"

"Let's just say I don't want any problems at this peace conference until I've had sufficient time to prepare an appropriate response."

I didn't like the sound of that, but if Ronan was in danger, I could deal with Vaughn after I made sure my boss was secure. I turned back to the bartender and told him to add my bill to the room tab before racing for the stairs. If I stopped at the elevator and waited for the car to come down, that would take longer than if I just ran up the few flights.

I took the steps two at a time, my heart racing. It was one thing for me to worry something might happen to Ronan, but something else entirely to be told he was in danger, especially by Vaughn. What if the vampire was just trying to stir up trouble? For all I knew, Ronan could be fine. I should've called up to the room, checked in with the guards. But there wasn't time now.

I burst through the double doors onto the floor with our suites and raced down the hall. Mark, on-shift alone to make Ronan feel less constrained in his own room, was sitting outside the suite door in a chair, a paperback novel in his hand. He immediately jumped up at my approach. "Ma'am! I mean, Callie! I thought… I mean…"

I didn't have time for his stammering. "When was the last time you did a visual check?"

Mark blinked. "But you said…"

I didn't wait for him to finish. I jerked the key out of my pocket, slid into the lock, and pulled open the door.

From the living area, everything looked to be in order. Nothing was out of place. Maybe Vaughn was wrong, or at least just misinformed. To be on the safe side, I went to Ronan's door and knocked.

The other side was silent.

I knocked again. "Ronan? It's me, Callie. I don't need to see you. Just need to hear your voice for a security check."

Silence.

I gestured to Mark behind me, and he handed over the suite's master key. With shaky hands, I unlocked the door and gripped the handle. "I'm coming in, so you'd better not be naked!" I pushed open the door. The room beyond was dark, but I didn't hear anyone breathing or moving. "Are you sure they were in here?" I asked Mark.

"Positive. I watched them both go in."

I flipped on the light, only to find the bedroom empty. Both Ronan and Olivia were gone.

CHAPTER NINE

I searched the room immediately, making notes on my phone for later. The bed looked undisturbed. Whatever they'd been doing in there, they'd never made it to the bed. I checked and found the locks on the windows secure, but the balcony door had been left open. It was hard to say if Ronan had left it that way or if someone had broken in. As far as I could tell, there were no signs of forced entry. No broken glass on the floor, and no signs of a struggle, at least at first glance.

I still held out hope that the two of them had just climbed down from the balcony and gone AWOL to escape prying eyes and ears. It didn't seem like the sort of thing Ronan would normally do, but then, he hadn't been acting like himself lately. Maybe Olivia was a bad influence. That was the best-case scenario.

The worst-case scenario was that someone had kidnapped them and hurt them, maybe even killed them. I pushed that thought away, not willing to think about it. There wasn't any blood on the floor, and Mark had reported no sounds or signs of a struggle, although he had not been in the suite. If anyone had attacked them, there would've been screaming. Ronan wasn't helpless either. He had magic too and could defend himself in a pinch.

No, even if something bad had happened to Ronan, whoever had him wouldn't kill him. He was a valuable prisoner. If this was a kidnapping, they'd hold on to him and demand a ransom. That had to be it. Ronan had money, and he didn't make a secret of that. Anyone, supernatural or not, could exploit a wealthy man for money.

The first thing I did was dial Ronan's number on my phone. I chewed my fingernails as I held the phone to my ear, listening to it ring. *Come on, Ronan. Pick up.*

A familiar ringtone started somewhere in the room, muffled but definitely there. With panic building in my stomach, I turned to the drawers to rifle through them. Maybe he'd just tucked it away and forgotten to take it with him. The drawers, however, were empty of any electronic devices, and the phone continued to ring. I pulled the blankets off the bed and pushed aside the mattress. Still no phone. It wasn't until I looked under the bed that I found it.

I retrieve the phone from where it lay face-down under the bed with a grunt and sat up. The screen was cracked, my name on the incoming call screen barely readable. Something definitely wasn't right. Ronan would never leave without his phone, and if he had damaged it, he would've told me, even if we weren't speaking. Ronan's phone was his lifeline to the rest of the world, and without it, he wouldn't know what to do with himself half the time. There wasn't an hour that passed by where he wasn't taking a selfie, checking his social media, or sending an email to someone. It was the first sign that he and Olivia hadn't left of their own accord.

Since the bed was already halfway taken apart, I pulled the box springs away from the headboard. There I found one of Olivia's bright red shoes. Unless they'd decided to run around Paris barefoot and the other shoe was somewhere else in the room, I was now sure they hadn't just snuck out.

As I was pondering what to do, there was a commotion at the door. I left Ronan's bedroom and found Mark and Yvonne arguing with Vaughn at the entrance to the suite. "Let him in." I gestured for them to step aside.

"Thank you," Vaughn said, buttoning his jacket and stepping into the suite. "It's good to know someone still has a little sense."

I held up a hand, preventing him from going farther. "You're going to tell me how you knew Ronan was in danger. Everything. No games, Vaughn."

Vaughn leaned to the side, trying to see around me into the bedroom. "Something's happened, hasn't it?"

I crossed my arms. "I'm not going to say more, and you're not taking another step until you answer my question. How did you know?"

The vampire studied me, the lower half of his face drooping into a frown. "I meant what I said earlier, Ms. Hart. I mean you and your employer no harm. I swear to you that I was not a part of any of this."

"Just get to the point."

He pursed his lips, considering. "I have been monitoring certain radio broadcasts since my arrival in Paris yesterday. Earlier this morning, I noted an uptick in activity on one of those. I instructed my people to monitor it more closely and to let me know if anything interesting came of it. A short while before I came to find you in the bar, my people reported a mostly jumbled communication. They did, however, note a name: Ronan McAllister."

"It would have been nice if you had shared that information with me from the start." If I'd known about the radio broadcasts, I would've had my team listening to them. Someone besides Vaughn should've been monitoring them. I couldn't be the only one who didn't know.

Vaughn folded his hands behind his back and stood up straighter. "The channels have been primarily used for private communication between different groups of vampires in the past. The specific channel we were monitoring is an unused one, or at least one that is not officially used. I do not believe people using it are vampires, but rather people who know about the channels and would know that specific one was not in use currently."

So, in other words, someone who knew about the peace celebration, but he didn't want to point the finger at any vampires. If it wasn't the vampires, however, who could it be? Who else had any motive whatsoever to kidnap Ronan? There were the hotel employees, I supposed, or anyone who knew the celebration was taking place. It wasn't like it was a secret. Sure, the average citizen had no idea the attendees were fae and vampires, but considering the locale and the expense, even an idiot could work out that the attendees were all rich. Ronan might've been a target of opportunity, rather than a specifically chosen target. I needed to know more to draw any conclusions.

"I'm going to need to know everything your people know about the broadcast," I said to Vaughn. "Sooner rather than later."

Vaughn nodded. "I can give you restricted access. Transcribed documents and perhaps some recordings, but only after my people have removed any confidential information."

That was going to take a while. Longer than I had to wait. I needed to find Ronan ASAP. The longer he was missing, the higher the chance that something bad would happen to him. Not only that but if Mab found out, she'd send her knight after me for letting it happen. We had to wrap this up quickly and quietly, and I'd have to do it without access to Vaughn's recordings. At least for now.

Sam knocked on the doorframe. "Tour ended early and since you sounded like you wanted to get together, I came right back. The guards told me what's going on. Any news?"

I shook my head. "I found his phone and one of her shoes, but that's it."

"That doesn't sound encouraging."

"Tell me something I don't know," I mumbled.

They came into the bedroom to put their arms around me and squeezed gently. "I'm sorry this happened, Callie. Don't blame yourself. It's not your fault. You couldn't have known. No one could've."

I squeezed Sam back. "I should have. I warned him that he wasn't behaving responsibly. I should've been up here on staff. This was supposed to be my shift, but I gave it away. Well, I would have been off by now, but still."

There was a part of me that wanted to be mad at Mark,

but it wasn't his fault either. He couldn't have done anything other than what he did. I'd given him instructions, and he'd followed them to the letter. Would I have heard the struggle if I had stayed behind? Maybe, maybe not. Maybe I would've dismissed it as the two of them doing the horizontal tango. It was hard to say and pointless to speculate. Though my mind wanted to look for someone or something to blame, it'd have to wait until we found who was behind all this.

I yelped when something buzzed in my pocket. It took me entirely too long to realize it was my phone. I'd tucked it away shortly after locating Ronan's.

"Who is it?" Sam asked as I fished it out.

I stared at the screen, frowning. There was no number, only a word—one I didn't like. "I don't know. It says 'restricted.'" With my heart beating in my throat, I slid my thumb over the screen and lifted the phone to my ear. "Hello?"

A garbled and heavily filtered voice came through. "I have the man you're looking for."

"Ronan? Are you saying you took him?" The room stilled at my words, the guards ceasing their search. Sam held their breath. Vaughn turned all his attention to me.

"Yes," said the voice.

They weren't idiots, whoever they were. We were dealing with professionals, people who knew not to say more than was absolutely necessary. That was a good sign. Professionals were much less likely to make a mistake like hurting him.

I swallowed and shifted the phone against my ear. "Prove it."

The phone creaked and filled with static for a moment. Was it because they were moving, or because they had transferred the call somewhere else?

"Callie?"

I couldn't stop myself from letting out a relieved breath at the sound of Ronan's voice.

"Callie," Ronan continued, "I'm not hurt. I'm okay."

The phone creaked again before the other voice came back on. "If you want them to stay okay, you're going to do everything I say exactly as I say when I say to do it. You will not contact the police. You will not alert anyone else at the hotel. Not the management, not any of the other guests. If I even suspect that you talked, I'll start cutting things off. Things they will miss."

Olivia suddenly screeched in the background. There was all the proof I needed that this wasn't personal. They thought I gave a damn about her. If they were smart, if they had done the research, they would know they should be threatening Ronan and not his random fling.

However, I wasn't just going to leave her behind. No matter how I felt about her personally, she was still a human being, and she was in danger too. I had to get them both out of there.

"You got it," I said, nodding. "Just tell me what you want."

"It won't be that easy. First, I need to know that you're taking this seriously. I'll call back with further instructions."

I tried to get them to stay on the line, but they hung up.

I lowered the phone and turned Vaughn. "Anything useful in that?"

He shrugged. "They sounded like professionals to me. Idiots, but people who've clearly done this before. If I were to give you advice, it would be to pay the ransom and move on. Getting the police or any other authorities involved will just complicate things. Besides, don't rich people like Ronan have kidnapping insurance or something?" He gestured vaguely to the air.

I had no idea if he did or not. Either way, he had plenty of cash in reserve, and I was authorized to make any withdrawals necessary. Unfortunately, Mab also had access to Ronan's funds and monitored them regularly. If I pulled out a large sum of money, it might trigger an alert. Next thing I knew, I'd be getting a call from the winter queen, asking me why I made a million-dollar withdrawal. Or however much the kidnappers asked for.

My fingers tightened around the phone. "So, you're saying I should just sit on my hands for the next hour and do nothing? Let those assholes get away with it?"

Vaughn folded his arms. "My people run retrieval jobs like this on occasion. Rescue a kidnapped dignitary or recover stolen goods. You don't want to know what our success rate is, but I'll tell you anyway—it's incredibly low. Sadly, even as low as it is, it's one of the highest in the industry. Most kidnappers or thieves will not do anything stupid as long as they think they'll get what they want. As long as all they asked for is money..." He shrugged again. "You can always track them down after the fact."

As much as I hated to admit it, Vaughn was right. Ronan and Olivia would be safer if I just gave the kidnappers what they wanted. Provided what they wanted didn't get anyone else hurt, I didn't see that I had a choice. Whatever happened afterward, we could deal with it. Even if Mab found out, I'd rather have her angry at me for handing money over to the kidnappers than have Ronan get hurt.

I crossed the room to pick up Ronan's phone charger and plugged my phone in. "Then I guess we wait," I said. "Until the kidnapper calls back, no one leaves this suite."

CHAPTER TEN

Despite my promise to wait for further instructions and just give the kidnappers what they wanted, I went back to my room and started prepping for the rescue mission. I knew enough about the situation to be suspicious. Sometimes kidnappers said they wanted money, but if I showed up with a briefcase full of cash, there was always the chance they would grab me too. They could haul me back to wherever they were holding Ronan and Olivia and call Mab and demand even more. Anything could happen, and I needed to be prepared for the worst.

I laid all of my equipment out on the bed and started strapping things to me one by one, starting with the body armor. It went on under my button-up, which made the shirt almost too small, but if I left it untucked, I could get away with it. Anyone who looked at me for more than a few seconds would know I was wearing body armor, and it wouldn't protect me from headshots, but it was better than nothing.

Next, I selected two handguns, simple pistols without

any bells or whistles, since they would fit better in concealed places. I swapped out my regular shoes for a pair of boots and slid a small knife down the side of one of them. My hair went up in a tight bun, which I fastened with a pair of sharpened wooden chopsticks—good for fighting in a pinch, but not the most practical. They were weapons of last resort unless there were vampires waiting for me. In that case, they might make great impromptu stakes.

I was in the middle of securing my belt when Sam came through the door. "Damn, Rambo. Or should I call you Callie Hart, vampire hunter?"

"Very funny." I lifted my boot to the edge of the bed so I could tighten the laces.

"You're not seriously going out like that, are you?"

"You think it's too much?"

Sam crossed their arms and frowned, touching their chin and looking me up and down. "They'll probably pat you down as soon as they show up. That's what I'd do, anyway, and I'm not even a professional."

Sam had a point. I finished tightening the laces on my boots and turned to the mirror to look at myself. I had definitely gone overboard. Maybe I didn't need the two pistols after all. Everything else I could probably get away with. Just to be safe, I threw on a leather jacket. The material was thick enough that it would be difficult for a vampire to bite through. To protect my neck, I turned up the collar.

Sam snickered. "Now you look like a movie star from an eighties action flick."

"I'll be back," I intoned in my best Terminator voice.

Sam eased into the loveseat, picking up the stuffed owl and holding it on their lap. "What about Vaughn's advice to just give them what they want?"

"It's been almost an hour, and they haven't called. We still don't know what they want. Money is the best-case scenario. What if they're using Ronan to blackmail me into doing something? What if I show up with the money and they attack me? We don't know what's going to happen, so I have to be prepared for anything."

They nodded. "Hope for the best, prepare for the worst. Got it. What are you going to do if they don't call?"

I didn't have an answer, or at least not a satisfying one. Paris was a big city, and one I didn't know. Even if I had someone with me who could translate, getting around the city wouldn't be easy. And that was to say nothing of the undercity. Finding one man in a city of millions would be impossible.

I didn't even know for sure that he was still in Paris. In the time Ronan had been gone, they could've put him on a bus, train, or plane to anywhere in the world. If they had taken him out of Paris, there was zero chance I'd be able to find him.

"Dammit, I knew I should have implanted a GPS tracker under his skin," I mumbled to myself.

Sam blinked. "Okay, even I think that's a little far, Callie. Are you okay?"

"Well, it'd make all of this easier, wouldn't it?"

They shrugged. "I have to agree, but Ronan is not a dog."

"Still, if he had listened to me, we wouldn't be in this mess." I sank onto the bed and collapsed backward, staring at the ceiling. "It just frustrates me that he doesn't listen to me. The guy hired me to do a job, and then he won't listen to the advice I give him. The advice he pays me to give him."

"What's that line about leading a horse to water and forcing it to drink?" The bedsprings squeaked and the mattress shifted as Sam moved to sit next to me. "There's also a balance to be had between being safe and having fun. If you spend your entire life safe, you'll miss out on a lot. The same is true of the opposite. If you ignore safety in favor of doing whatever you want, you're likely to have something bad happen to you. The problem you and Ronan have is that you want to live at different extremes. You want everyone to believe you're perfectly happy, living a safe, boring life. Ronan wants everyone to believe he's ready to throw caution to the wind at a moment's notice. He's so desperate to prove he can make his own decisions that he's not making smart ones all the time. And you, you're so afraid of getting hurt that you won't let yourself endure a moment of vulnerability."

I sat up and blinked at Sam, who was staring off the distance, hugging their stuffed owl to their chest. "Damn. Didn't expect that sort of insight out of you."

Sam grinned and tilted their head toward me. "Must be that interpersonal psychology course I took last semester. It's true, though, isn't it? If you guys could meet some-where in the middle, you might find that you're both a little right and both a little wrong."

Sam was more right than they'd ever been. For years, I'd kept everyone at arm's length because that was easier and safer. Jax's betrayal had driven that point home. If I couldn't trust my brothers in arms, who could I trust? I didn't have any family. Aside from Sam, I didn't really have friends. Relationships had always been hard for me. I had decided a long time ago that I was better off looking after myself. It was part of the reason I joined the Army in the first place. I went to war to learn how to defend myself, and in doing so, was honored to have the opportunity to defend my country. But maybe it was time to lower my defenses a little. Maybe that was why I was so drawn to Kai. It was easy to do that with him, almost natural. If only I could do the same with other people.

There was a knock at the door. I hopped up from the bed and rushed to the suite entrance. I was expecting Vaughn's people to arrive with the tape transcripts. I didn't know how helpful they'd be, but it was better than sitting around doing nothing, which was what it felt like I was doing. Instead, I found Kai on the other side of the door.

"I came by to see if you still wanted to go to dinner," he said.

I leaned on the door, blocking his view of the rest of the suite. "Now is not really a good time."

"Oh," he said somewhat awkwardly. "Are you on duty?"

"Sort of." Maybe he can help, I thought. Kai was the summer Knight, which meant he had resources. Ronan and the rest of the winter court might not be happy about his involvement, but the truth was I needed help, and he could give it. I opened the door a little wider. "Actually, I have a problem you might be able to help me with."

Kai stepped in and paused when he saw all the other security roaming about. "Is something going on?"

"You have to promise not to tell anyone."

"You have my word as the summer knight," he said. "Anything you tell me will not leave this room."

I took a deep breath. "Ronan's been kidnapped."

"Wow, that's not what I was expecting you to say. Does Mab know?"

"No, and I'd like to keep it that way."

He nodded. "I see. How can I help?"

I fidgeted with my hands for a moment. "Honestly, I don't know yet. I'm expecting a call from the kidnappers any minute. If you could just be here, that might be enough."

"Of course, Callie. Whatever you need."

I was in the middle of thanking him when the phone rang. I broke off mid-word and headed to where the phone was plugged in, scrambling to answer. "Hello?"

"The American Cathedral. One hour. One million Euros. Cash." It was the same garbled mechanical voice from before, and they hung up as soon as they finished speaking.

I lowered the phone.

"Well?" Kai asked. "What did they say?"

I turned around. "Do you know where the American Cathedral is?"

"Is that where the exchange is supposed to take place?"

I nodded.

"I can take you there in a rental car. It's not that far."

"They said to tell no one, but they won't know." I turned to address the rest of my team. "I'm going to go make the exchange. Yvonne, if I'm not back by the end of the day, you're in charge. I want you to call the police and tell them what's happened."

"Should we tell Natalie and the other vampires?" Jim asked.

I hesitated. On the one hand, they should know their venue wasn't secure. On the other, I didn't want to cause a stir. Vaughn had left, promising to keep what he knew to himself as long as I did. If I broke my word to him, there was no telling what he'd do. He was acting unpredictably, just like everyone else. Should I at least update him? I could call using the Meyer Securities number, but did I want him involved? I decided I didn't. He might come in all guns blazing and blow the whole thing. "No," I said finally. "Not unless you have to."

Sam came to squeeze the air out of my lungs in another big hug. "Be careful, Callie. Don't take any stupid risks."

I patted their arm. "Stay here until I get back, huh? Last thing I need is to be tracking you through Paris."

They agreed. With no more preparations to see to, I followed Kai out the door. Letting him take me might be a bad idea—I didn't precisely trust him, although I was leaning that way for no reason I could explain—and I didn't know what would be waiting for me at the cathedral, but I wasn't leaving there without Ronan.

CHAPTER ELEVEN

There were a lot of cathedrals in Paris. Most of them dated back hundreds of years, but the one where the kidnappers had told me to meet them was only about a hundred and sixty years old, give or take a few. It was the oldest English-speaking church in Paris, however, and part of the Anglican Communion, all of which I learned in a few minutes online during the drive over.

I wouldn't have called it a sprawling Gothic-style cathedral, but more Gothic-inspired. It looked too white, too clean, and too new to fit the first description, although it did have tall, pointed rooftops, huge stained glass windows, columns, and jagged points. The pale bell tower reached up to stand twice as tall as the rest of the building. The exterior must've felt right at home against a backdrop of both cobbled brick streets and passing cars. It was the perfect blend of old and modern.

Getting a million Euros hadn't been easy, even with access to Ronan's account. When I went in to make the withdrawal, I'd had to talk to the branch manager and sign some papers. The kidnappers had only given me a one-hour window to show up, and that time was ticking away fast.

Kai pulled the rental car over a block from the church. I leaned out my window to give the building a better look. Worry churned in my stomach. Was Ronan inside, or were they keeping him somewhere else? Should I make the exchange if I didn't see him? Probably not. If I handed them the money before I had Ronan in my sights, they might just take the cash and run. Then I'd be right back where I started and have to come up with more money.

The duffel bag full of cash sat awkwardly at my feet. In the movies, the people making the exchange always had an expensive briefcase. I'd tried to find one, but Ronan was the only one among us that even owned a briefcase, and his was back in Ohio. In the end, I'd dumped out the duffel bag I'd brought with me to Paris and shoved the cash in that. Why was I sitting there, glued to my seat with my heart drumming against my ribcage?

"Do you want me to go in with you?" Kai asked.

I shook my head. The kidnappers hadn't said to come alone, but they *had* said during our first conversation that I shouldn't tell anyone. If Kai came in, I'd have to hope they'd buy whatever explanation I offered. Chances were good they'd be spooked at the sight of him and call the whole exchange off.

Not wanting to explain all that, I just said, "No, I've got this." My fingers closed around the rough fabric handles of the duffel bag. A small strip of Velcro bit into my palm with its tiny teeth.

Kai put a hand on my shoulder, stopping me from

getting out of the car. "I'll pull around the block and wait at the back of the cathedral, okay? Be careful, Callie. I don't want you to get hurt."

I didn't look at him, afraid if I did, I'd become as worried about doing this as he seemed to be. "I'm going to be fine, Kai. Just wait for me around back, like you said."

The air outside was warm, though a chilly wind swept through the street, pushing stray hairs against the side of my face. I shifted my grip on the duffel bag as I walked toward the church. It was surprisingly light, considering the amount of cash inside. I thought a million Euros would be a lot more bills than it was. There were a few pedestrians on the sidewalk, but none of them paid attention to me or what I was doing. Still, I could swear I felt eyes on the back of my head all the way to the building.

Upon entering the cathedral, I had to pause for a minute to take in the beauty. I'd dismissed the outside as just another nineteenth-century church, but inside, it was a work of art. The stained glass windows that had seemed so simple from the outside cast a rainbow of colors over rows of wooden pews in the sanctuary visible through large, open doors. The hallway where I stood wrapped around the sanctuary, branching off into other chapels along the sides. There was a small fountain and a stand with a large book. A pen was chained to the stand. It looked like a guest book, but I didn't stop to check it out. Signs above my head pointed to restrooms in the corner one way and church offices in the other direction.

After a brief pause in the entry, I put on a mask of calm confidence and walked into the sanctuary. I'd expected it to be empty on a weekday afternoon. Instead, there were about a dozen people spread throughout the pews, all focused forward. I paused at the back of the sanctuary, scanning the crowd and wondering which one of those people was my contact. They hadn't given me specific instructions about who I was to wait for. Rather than approach a random person, I slid into the third pew from the front on the right, as far as I could get from everyone else. I didn't want to disturb anyone who might be praying. The duffel bag went on the seat next to me with my arm looped through the handles.

As I waited, I couldn't help but glance at my watch. There were only a few minutes left in the hour. What if my watch was slow and I'd missed the window? Just to be sure, I checked my phone and fiddled with the dials on my watch to make sure the times matched. Then I put the phone away and nervously tapped my foot for a minute before I caught myself and stopped. I had to look anything but nervous. Nervous people attracted attention, and I didn't need to be approached by anyone other than the kidnappers.

Someone slid into the pew behind me. I started to turn around but paused when he said, "Don't turn around. Keep your eyes forward."

My eyes snapped to the front of the sanctuary.

"Very good," said the man. "Did you come alone?"

"Does it look like I brought backup?" I tipped my head to the side and strained my eyes to try to make out any details that might help me track him down later. I wasn't letting these assholes get away with kidnapping Ronan. "Where's Ronan?"

"Put the bag of money on the floor and slide it under the pew with your foot."

"Not until I see Ronan."

"That's not how this works." He had an accent, but not a French one. Where was he from? I couldn't place it, no matter how hard I tried. His English was perfect, though. "First, you give me the money. Then I count it. If the amount in the bag matches the amount I'm expecting, I will make a phone call. My friends on the other end will release your friend, and our business will be over."

Ronan's not here. For all I know, releasing him meant pushing him into a volcano or out of an airplane seven miles up. My hand tightened around the bag strap. "The way I see it, I'm the one with the bargaining power here. How about you tell me where Ronan is, and *then* I give you the money?"

"Don't push me."

"At least give me proof you have him. You could be a scammer for all I know, or not involved at all." I turned my head a little farther. He wore a blue suit.

"Eyes forward!"

I turned my head forward. *Keep him talking, Callie. The more he says, the more he gives away, and the closer I get to finding Ronan.* "Come on. It's a reasonable request. Prove to me you have him, and I'll do everything else you ask."

He was silent for a long moment before he snorted. "I'll have to clear this with my employer."

He was just a middleman, but he knew where Ronan was. I listened, waiting for his clothing to rustle as he searched his pockets for a cell phone. I gave him just enough time to get distracted by dialing before I turned in the pew and launched myself over it, swinging the duffel bag as I did. Surprised cries echoed through the sanctuary, but the kidnapper just grunted as the bag clobbered him in the face. It wasn't heavy, but I swung it with enough force to sting. He jerked to one side, momentarily stunned. I capitalized on that, landing a hard punch to his nose. It broke with a crunch.

By that time, most people had gotten up out of their seats to either flee in terror or retrieve their cell phones to record our fight. The kidnapper was so stunned, I was able to drag him out of the pew and held him up, facing the nearest phone. "Smile for the camera. Our faces are probably going to be on the evening news."

He tried to pry my hands free from his jacket, but I had too good a hold on it. When he realized that, he tried to slip out of the jacket. I helped him, yanking the jacket back and folding it over his head. Try to get out of that.

"Help!" screamed the kidnapper. "Someone help!"

I slung the duffel bag over a shoulder and dragged him toward the hall. He struggled all the way down the hall and even as I dragged him into the bathroom. "Quit fighting, asshole, or I'll break something else."

"Don't kill me!"

I rolled my eyes and shoved him into the nearest stall with a grunt. "I'm not going to kill you. I'm going to interrogate you." I yanked the jacket off him. "Where's Ronan?"

He blinked up at me, his eyes starting to swell from the broken nose. "Nobody was supposed to get hurt!"

"Well, that was before you tried to play hardball with me. Where is he?" I made a fist.

He flinched and waved his hands. "I don't know! I was just sent to make the exchange."

"Last chance. Where is he?"

The guy's demeanor suddenly changed, his face hardening. He spat at me. "Fuck you, lady! I'm not telling you anything!"

I grabbed him, hauled him away from the toilet, and shoved his face under the automatic hand dryer, switching it on. He growled as the side of his face heated up, turning bright red. I waited for it to turn off before asking him again.

I got the distinct feeling he was about to tell me where I could shove my questions when we were interrupted by the door swinging open. Three more guys in suits filed into the bathroom. One of them turned to lock the bathroom door behind him.

I let go of the guy I was interrogating. "Something tells me you guys aren't here for the holy water."

The closest one flipped open a switchblade and swung it at me. I caught his arm and sent a surge of magic down into it. I'd been practicing with Ronan once a week, learning how to control it. It was difficult, and I hadn't made much progress, the power still out of reach about half the time. This time, though, it answered. The attacker's arm froze solid. He stared at it and backed away, screaming.

Another one took a swing at me. I dodged out of the way and let his fist connect with the first guy. He hit him in the chin and laid him out on the bathroom floor, out cold. Enraged, he turned to me, but I was busy dealing with his friend, who'd jumped in to tackle me. I'd moved out of the way just in time, and he only managed to wrap himself around one of my legs.

"Get off!" I shouted and kicked him repeatedly in the shoulder and the side of the head.

The kidnapper with the broken nose and the burned face was back on his feet now, making it three against one. Those weren't great odds, but I liked three to one a hell of a lot better than four to one.

I finally kicked the one off my leg and tried to go for the knife I had hidden in my boot, but they didn't give me time. Two of them swung at me at once. I backed against the wall between two sinks, deflecting one blow and turning to take the second in the back rather than the ribs. With a shout, I grabbed one, wrenched, and turned, shoving him into the other. Both tumbled into a stall. One of them hit the toilet tank with a loud bang and was still while the other hit the wooden divider wall hard enough to go through it.

That left me facing off with the kidnapper with the broken nose since the one with the frozen arm was still out of it. He blinked, looked at his groaning and fallen friends, and decided he'd rather run than go another round with me. He rushed for the bathroom door, tore open the lock, and fled.

I looked around the broken bathroom, wincing at the damage. Better get out of here before someone comes to bill me for the damages, but where to? I still didn't have Ronan, and the kidnapper hadn't given me much to go on.

Maybe not, but he's still out there, running. If I were a bad guy who just got my ass kicked by a girl, where would I run to? Wherever I felt safe. He'd probably go straight to wherever they were keeping Ronan, which wasn't a smart move. The guy didn't strike me as overly intelligent. All I had to do was track him there.

I picked up the duffel bag full of money and slung it over my shoulder. "Well, fellas, it's been fun, but let's not do this again," I said and pushed through the bathroom door.

CHAPTER TWELVE

The money man with the broken nose had a nice head start, but his injuries slowed him down. He must have been at least slightly disoriented because it took him a while to find his way out of the church. I could've caught up to him on the street out front, but decided against it. Good thing too, since a couple of police cars pulled in as soon as I walked away from the front door. There was a small crowd of people in front of the church, mostly folks who hadn't been in the sanctuary when I grabbed the kidnapper. They must have just joined the herd stampeding out of the church. I disappeared into the throng of people, tucking my head low and putting my hands in my pockets. As long as I didn't walk too fast or do anything to draw attention, I could get away clean.

No one stopped the kidnapper I was tailing or me. He walked to the end of the block and tried to hail a cab, but no one would stop for him, not with the street blocked off. So he wouldn't see me, I ducked into the mouth of an alley and waited for him to give up, which didn't take long. After looking around one more time, he went up the cross street. I stepped out of the alley to follow him, making sure to give him plenty of distance.

Following someone was easy if you knew how to do it. The tricky part was not getting close enough to alert them. It was easier to pull off if the person you were following traveled through a crowded space, but you risked losing him there too. In empty streets and alleys, the best way was to stay just far enough behind them that you came around a corner at the same time he went around the next. If he slowed down, you slowed down. If he sped up, you had to match his pace.

The kidnapper led me away from the church and farther into Paris, away from any of the main areas. As I followed, I considered calling Kai or Sam to tell them where I was going. Problem was, I didn't know. I didn't know for certain where I was, even in relation to the church. The kidnapper had taken so many turns already that I was lost. My only hope of finding Ronan now was to follow him and not getting caught. Kai would figure it out.

Like any large city, Paris had its neighborhoods, and I wasn't well-versed enough in the local scene to know which ones were safe and which might be dangerous. It wasn't obvious at first glance, either, because the buildings generally seemed well-maintained. Graffiti gradually appeared more frequently on the walls, and I saw more cars with their windows smashed or up on blocks. The buildings were narrower and crammed closer together, and loud music was more frequent.

I tried to avoid being seen, but it couldn't be helped. I must've looked out of place in my heavy jacket with the black duffel bag over my shoulder. No one stopped the man I was following to offer help for his bloody nose, and no one stopped me to ask me what was in the bag. In a way, I was safer walking through the bad neighborhoods than the affluent ones. No one in a high-crime area was going to call the police to report two odd-looking strangers roaming around.

Eventually, the sun made me want to shrug off the jacket because it was making me sweat. It was the only thing giving me any anonymity, though, so I left it on. As I walked, I worked out in my head what I might say if someone did stop me. I thought I'd pretend to be in a hurry to get somewhere until I realized everyone in the neighborhood probably spoke French. I wouldn't be able to pretend I belonged, and as soon as anyone pegged me for a tourist, they'd think I was helpless. I'd have a fight on my hands. A fight would slow me down and allow time for the guy I was following to escape. I couldn't afford a fight, so I set a scowl on my face and tried to look threatening so people would give me a wide berth. So far, it'd worked.

After what felt like forever, the residential neighborhoods faded and we walked back into a commercial area. The guy I was following slowed his pace and took far fewer turns than he had in the residential areas. Maybe he thought he was safe and that he had lost anyone following him by now. He was wrong. I was still hot on his tail, and closer than ever to finding Ronan. And when I did, boy, was he going to get an earful from me.

He suddenly turned away from the sidewalk and ducked into a subway station. I sped up to follow. Crowds were pouring out, which would make it easier to lose him.

Closing the distance would prevent that, or at least make it less likely. I crested the stairs as soon as he stepped off. Dammit, somehow he'd put more distance between us than I'd anticipated. I sped down the stairs, taking them two at a time. When I reached the bottom, I searched for him but came up empty until I spied him slipping through the turnstile. I didn't have a pass, so I had to pause to pay. It was tempting to break into Ronan's money on my back. I had, after all, been hauling it all over the city for more than an hour now, and I felt like I deserved to have him pay for his own rescue, but I didn't want to open the bag in front of everyone. I used one of my credit cards and slid through the turnstile, hoping he hadn't yet gotten on a train.

There were two platforms, both crowded. Neither had a train waiting, and from the sounds of it, none had departed in the last thirty seconds or so. That meant he was still there somewhere. I just had to locate the right platform. I searched the upper one and came up empty, so I descended the second set of stairs to the bottom platform. From above, I hadn't spotted him there either, but maybe the cement column was blocking my view.

It was as I was coming down the stairs that I located him again, standing on the lower platform, but on the other side. I ducked behind a heavyset man waiting for the train so he wouldn't see me and waited between him and the cement column.

A subway train hissed into the station a few short moments later. I peeked around the column, but I couldn't tell if he'd gotten on. Time to take a chance. I followed the heavyset man onto a car and sat down next to him. A moment later, the money man climbed into the same car. I shrank into the seat as far as possible, hoping he wouldn't notice me.

The subway trundled along noisily, jerking back and forth as it sped along the rails. The station announcements were in French, English, and German, but they weren't helpful to me since I didn't know where he was getting off. I had to covertly lean forward and glance at the man on the other side of the subway car before every stop to see if he was getting up.

The man I was following seemed settled in for a long ride. I hoped the guy next to me didn't get off too soon, or I'd lose what little cover I had. He might spot me. I searched for anything to hide my face, but all I had was my bag. He'd seen the bag, though, so I hid it next to me. The best I could do was lower my head and hide my face behind the upturned collar of my jacket.

As the subway car slid into another stop, the big guy next to me stood. I stole a glance around him. My target was still seated, examining his reflection in the window. I needed to move so he wouldn't see me. I stood and clung to the big man as if we were related, following him out of the car. As soon as we stepped off onto the platform, the big guy turned on me and said something quick in French.

"Oh, sorry," I replied in English. "My mistake."

As soon as I spoke English, his attitude changed. "Ah, American. Are you lost?"

"I think I got off at the wrong stop." I waved at him, trying to be friendly, and got back on the subway train, one car behind where I'd been. I'd avoided detection for now, but changing cars meant I couldn't keep as close an eye on him. I'd have to pay very close attention at every stop.

Luckily, he got off at the next, and I spotted him easily since almost no one else got off there. I slipped out with the other random person who exited the car at that station and hurried to the nearby stairs, where I found a corner to watch from. If he started for the stairs, I'd rush up them ahead, but he stayed where he was as if he were waiting for another train. He glanced around for a few moments, then started walking along the platform, moving deeper into the subway tunnel. I gave him a few seconds' head start and rushed after him.

My footsteps echoed in the narrow tunnel, so I tried to time them with his. He didn't seem to notice anything amiss. Maybe I'd given him enough space that he didn't hear me. The walkway narrowed until it was practically a tightrope. One wrong step and I could fall onto the tracks, where a passing train would hit me. If he turned around, he'd spot me for sure.

I spied a small alcove between two large metal things that might've been vents and ducked between them just as he shifted to look behind him. From where I was, I could see him, and I prayed he couldn't see me. He must not have been able to because he didn't shout or come toward me. He reached for a service door and pulled it open with a grunt. The hinges groaned loudly and creaked as he closed it.

If I opened that door, he would hear it for sure. I emerged from my hiding spot and took a step toward it.

The loud rumbling of a train echoed down the tunnel. If I opened the door while the train was passing, the noise would cover the squeak of the hinges. It'd also mean I'd be in danger of getting hit, though. There would only be inches between me and the train until I dove through the door. What choice did I have?

I licked my lips and hurried down the narrow walkway, my hand on the latch. The train barreled around the curve and charged full speed ahead. I closed my eyes, jerked the door open, and threw myself into the narrow tunnel beyond. The train thundered by, so loud I could barely think.

When it was gone, I lowered my hands from my ears and turned to look down the tunnel. Steam vented into the narrow space, heating it to a sticky temperature that had to be in excess of a hundred degrees. I was immediately too hot and removed my jacket so I didn't overheat. There was no sign of the bagman, so I hurried down the tunnel, moving as silently as I could.

When I came to the first corner, I watched his shadow disappear around the next. Bingo. I followed him through the maze of narrow tunnels, his shadow just beyond my line of sight until I came to a crossroads. Ahead, the steam tunnels continued, but to the left, the ground tilted up toward the surface. On the right, it slanted down to a small wooden door that had once been chained shut. It was now unchained, but I didn't know if that was the way he went. With the steam hissing all around me, I couldn't hear any footfalls. The only thing I could do was make an educated guess.

I turned to the right and went through the chained door. The area on the other side was a small, round chamber with a large pipe in the center, big enough for a bear to fall through without touching any of the sides. Someone had dropped what looked like a homemade rope ladder from the side of the room, draping it down through the pipe. It wiggled as the bag man climbed down it. I could hear him brushing against the metal pipe below, and the splash as he jumped down. Judging by the smell, he'd descended into a sewer. I had to hurry if I didn't want to lose him.

The climb down the rope ladder felt like it lasted days. With no light, it was like I was descending into a never-ending pit. How the hell had they gotten Ronan and Olivia down there? Maybe they'd come another way. That had to be it. I couldn't imagine anyone dragging them this impossible distance, and certainly not down a rope ladder. The only way Ronan would've gone with anyone without fighting was if he was unconscious. He certainly wouldn't have let anyone harm an innocent like Olivia. Why *had* they taken Olivia, anyway? It would have been easier to get rid of her. Was she in on it? More questions, and no answers.

As I went down, my eyes adjusted to the light—either that or it gradually got brighter. I finally dropped into ankle-deep raw sewage and almost gagged. So much for that pair of boots. At least it wasn't a few inches higher, or it'd be splashing in and soaking my socks. I paused for a moment to make the loud plunk of my feet dropping into it had not been heard. No one came running, so I reasoned I must be safe.

Now to determine which way he went. I turned a full circle. There were two exits from the chamber, leading in opposite directions. Just by looking, I couldn't tell which way he went, but I could hear the faint sound of splashing. It echoed through the chamber, making it impossible to pinpoint without more work. Slowly, I moved first toward one opening and then the other, listening for the splashing sound and trying to guess which way to go.

It sounded slightly louder on one side, so that was the direction I went. Just through the opening, I found a slanted surface that led up out of the sewage to a narrow catwalk heading in the same direction. I took that rather than walk through more sewage. It didn't sound like that was the way the bagman had gone, but I was smarter than him, and he probably wasn't thinking clearly with a broken nose.

I followed the catwalk until it slanted back down into the sewage, but promptly stopped when I heard voices around the corner.

"—idiot!" shouted someone in English.

English?

"Sorry, boss. I did like you said." That was the voice of the man with the broken nose. He sounded awfully congested. "You said she'd follow directions, that this was low-risk. You could've told me she was a badass."

"She's his bodyguard, Clyde." The first voice again. Was it the echo, or did it sound familiar? "What did you expect? I told you not to take this lightly!"

"You also said she'd do as she was told to ensure his safety! You didn't see her. She was like a crazy lady! Jumped over the pew like an animal and shoved my face right at someone recording the fight."

"Someone recorded you? Dammit, Clyde. Your face is probably all over the city by now, if it hasn't been uploaded online somewhere. This is going to complicate things." The unknown voice moved closer, weakening the echo effect. "What about the others?"

"She beat them up."

"What?"

"Yeah, she dragged me to the bathroom and held my fucking face under a hand dryer! See? And then those three came in to stop her, and she kicked their asses. Froze Bobby's whole arm, Kai!"

Kai? A chill ran down my spine when I realized I *had* heard that voice somewhere before. It wasn't just familiar. That voice belonged to Kai, the summer knight.

CHAPTER THIRTEEN

I felt like an idiot. Everything he'd said and done had been an act so he could distract me and get close to Ronan, and I'd fallen for it. Not only that, but I'd provided him both an opportunity to act, and an alibi. Every moment he was with me, he knew I wasn't with Ronan, leaving him vulnerable. Not only that, but I'd messaged him earlier in the day to let him know I wasn't with Ronan. I'd practically put up a neon sign that said KIDNAP MY BOSS.

But why would Kai kidnap Ronan? It couldn't be about the money. I didn't know Kai's financial situation, but he didn't seem like he was hurting for cash. He'd thrown away a lot of money on an expensive bottle of wine we hadn't even finished the night before. Nothing about him struck me as someone who was in debt. What other reason would anyone have for kidnapping a prince?

Maybe it was politically motivated. Winter and summer weren't exactly enemies, but to call them allies was a stretch. There'd been open hostilities between the courts in the past, though that seemed like ancient history.

What if I'm the reason? It could be that Kai thought the only reason I hadn't jumped at the offer to join the summer court was my job with Ronan. If Ronan was out of the way, maybe I'd change my mind. And if he helped me rescue Ronan as he'd done, I might even see him in a more positive light, making me more likely to choose his side over Ronan's.

If that was the case, though, why ask for the ransom? He could just hold Ronan until I made up my mind, then release him. Was the whole ransom thing just a cover?

His shouting interrupted my thoughts. "Yes, it's as I thought. Look here. You're already up on YouTube. I'm sure they've identified you by now, and your name is probably all over the police scanners."

"Forget the local boys. If they pulled my file, they'll be on the phone with INTERPOL. I'm wanted in a few countries now. The heat's going to be on," said Clyde.

"It would seem so. I have no choice but to escalate my plans," Kai said.

"What do you want me to do, boss?"

"I don't know. Give me a minute to think. Call to check on the prisoners."

So, I thought from my hiding spot, they didn't bring Ronan and Olivia down here after all. They had them somewhere else. Guess Clyde was too smart to go straight there. This must just be his meeting spot with Kai.

A phone beeped, and a moment later, Clyde began speaking to whoever was on the other end. I didn't understand enough French to know what he was saying, but from his tone, it didn't sound good. "They're saying the woman is awake and won't stop screaming about bugs and spiders. They want permission to give her more sedative."

That must be how they'd moved them in the first place. I knew Ronan wouldn't go easy. I also had to admit I was laughing a little on the inside that Olivia was freaking out more about spiders and roaches than being kidnapped. Ronan sure could pick 'em.

"Absolutely not," Kai answered. "I don't trust those idiots not to overdose her."

"The girl's of no use to us. Who cares if she dies?"

"*I* care!" There was a loud thwack, presumably Kai smacking his underling for his stupidity. "No one dies. That's the whole point of this, isn't it? Tell them if they so much as think about... No, actually, give me the phone." There was a pause, followed by footsteps. "Now you listen to me. This job is half-botched already. Clyde blew the exchange. I don't need you two idiots screwing up on your end. Both Ronan and the woman remain safe." Another pause. "I don't care about that!" Pause. "If she's driving you crazy, find a gag. You're not injecting them again. I'm honestly surprised they're awake after the first one. That stuff can knock out a horse. Well, maybe she's hallucinating the bugs then. Like I said, it's a strong sedative. She might be having some sort of adverse reaction. Gag her, but monitor her breathing and make sure she doesn't develop a rash. I'll be there when I can. No more drugs without talking to me first, understand?"

The phone beeped again as he hung up.

"What now, boss?" Clyde asked.

The phone beeped some more as Kai punched in some numbers. "Now I fix your screw-up."

There was another long pause. I thought for a moment he might be texting someone or sending an email. Maybe there was another team handling another part of whatever scam Kai was running. Maybe he was talking to his queen. Surely he wouldn't pull this kind of thing without her approval?

That says a lot about the summer court, I thought. They suddenly didn't seem so warm and inviting.

My phone buzzed in my back pocket and suddenly erupted into song, a heavy metal guitar riff screaming through the opening of Metallica's *Master of Puppets*. Dammit, I'd forgotten to turn it off! I fumbled to grab it and shut off the ringtone, but it was too late. The damage was done.

A long silence followed, and for a moment, I held out hope that they'd dismissed it as an anomaly. It could happen, right?

Then I heard footsteps coming toward me.

I raced away, heading back up the tunnel with the sound of running footsteps behind me. At the ramp up to the catwalk, I lost some ground and the footsteps came closer, too close for comfort. Fingers brushed against my back, but I threw myself forward, tumbling down the catwalk into the sewage below.

It took a lot of mental effort to keep from vomiting, but I pushed myself up and sloshed through it, trying to remember which way I'd come.

Clyde's hand closed around the collar of my jacket, and he yanked me back. "Come here, you!"

I spun with a fist raised and clocked him one more time in the face. He let me go as fresh blood spurted from his nose and grabbed his injury. I turned to run away.

Kai suddenly jumped down from above to land in front of me with a loud splash. "Callie, there's no reason to run," he said, extending a hand. "I don't want to hurt you."

"That's what you said before too." I clenched both fists and widened my stance, preparing for a fight. I'd never seen Kai fight before, but he was the summer knight, so I had to assume he knew what he was doing.

"And you're not hurt." He inched toward me. "Are you?"

"No thanks to the thugs you sent after me. The church was a setup, wasn't it? What's the money for? Why take Ronan? Why jerk me around?"

"Everything will be clear in a few hours." He took another step.

From behind, Clyde wrapped his arms around me in a tight bear hug. I wrenched from side to side, trying to free myself, but he'd caught me off-guard, and his hold was too good.

While I was fighting Clyde, Kai stepped forward, pulling a needle from his pocket. "Don't fight, Callie. I promise it'll all be over soon."

I struggled as he jammed the needle into my neck. Even as blackness closed in at the edges of my vision, I did my best to fight. If I was going to go down, I was going to go down fighting.

In the end, it was pointless. My arms and legs refused to respond. My stomach surged into my throat, but I was suddenly too weak to swallow. I flopped over helplessly, saved from falling into the muck by the very man who'd betrayed me.

Kai passed me to Clyde. The last thing I heard before I lost consciousness was Kai telling Clyde, "Put her with the others."

CHAPTER FOURTEEN

My neck was sore, and my shoulders ached. Those were the first things I was aware of as I came to. With a groan, I lifted my head and tried to move my arms out of the awkward position they were in, only to find them zip-tied together behind me. That was unusual. I hadn't done anything that kinky in a while. No, wait, this is more serious than that. I realized I was sitting in a very uncomfortable wooden chair. The air around me was moist, with a strong undercurrent of sewage.

Someone was sobbing in between shrieks and panicked pleas in French.

Olivia? I thought at first they might be torturing her for some reason, although I couldn't imagine why. When I opened my eyes and they adjusted to the light, however, I realized she was sitting in a chair not far from me. Not a soul was near her, and nothing seemed to be happening.

"Cockroaches," Ronan said from the other side of me. "Little ones, I think. An hour ago, it was some kind of beetle."

I turned my head. "Ronan! Thank God you're okay!"

"'Okay' is relative. I've had to listen to her shrieking for hours, and it's driving me insane. You wait. You've only just arrived."

He had a point. I'd only been awake for a minute, and she was already getting on my nerves.

I shifted my shoulders, testing the strength of the zip-ties. Plastic. Breaking those wouldn't be easy in my position. "You're not hurt, though?"

"Well, I was hungry until they brought you in," Ronan said dryly. "No offense, Callie, but you reek of raw sewage."

"Yeah, I kind of fell into some while I was tailing a guy." I tried to pull my wrists apart, but all that did was dig the plastic into my skin. I winced.

"Tailing a guy?"

"Yeah, to save you."

Olivia's whimpering ramped up, and she started wiggling her chair back and forth, more frantic.

"Stop it!" I growled at her. "I can't think when you're doing that!"

She stopped moving but didn't let up her frantic sobbing. "They are on me! One crawled up my leg."

I supposed I'd be a little uncomfortable with a cockroach crawling on me, too, but screaming about it wasn't going to change anything. We needed to figure out how to get out of there and that required thinking through our situation, something I couldn't do with her being so noisy.

I turned my attention back to Ronan, ignoring Olivia for the moment. "Have you tried magic?"

He nodded. "It was one of the first things I tried. Magic doesn't seem to work in here for some reason."

"Is that possible? Is there some way Kai could have constructed something to shut it down? Keep us from using our powers?"

Ronan tilted his head to the side. "Maybe. He'd have to know the extent of our powers, though. My abilities are well known as the winter prince. However, he might not know very much about yours. You might be able to use your magic when I couldn't."

I cleared my throat, closed my eyes, and lowered my head, resting my chin against my chest in concentration. I'd been working on accessing my magic on command, but hadn't yet mastered that aspect. Like I said, it only worked about half the time, and since I had used it earlier in the day, I didn't expect it to work now. Sometimes, though, I could be surprised. It would take immense concentration and probably longer than usual, considering how badly my head was swimming. Whatever drug Kai had given me to knock me out must've been a doozy. I felt like I had just gotten over the worst hangover of my life. My skull was practically vibrating.

I reached for the magic deep within me. I could feel it there, lurking just out of reach, dormant. If I could just say the right thing or take the right action, it would wake and obey me. Unfortunately, I didn't know what the right thing was. Ronan and I had been going through exercises, trying to pin down a method that worked for me. So far, nothing had been particularly reliable. Trying to coax my magic to life with the splitting headache I was nursing didn't seem to be the key either. Olivia's sniffling didn't help.

"Ronan," I ground out through clenched teeth, "tell her to shut the hell up or I will."

He sighed. "I can try, but the last couple of times I've tried to get through to her, she didn't respond. I think she might be having some sort of a nervous breakdown."

"A nervous breakdown." I scoffed. "They're just bugs." I mean, yeah, they were gross bugs, and I wouldn't want them all over me, but he wouldn't see me freaking out over a couple of roaches. "I need quiet to concentrate, and she's ruining that. If you want to get out of here, shut her up."

"Olivia," Ronan said in a gentle whisper. He repeated her name three times before her whimpering died down slightly. I have no idea what he said next because he said in French, but it sounded soothing to me. He spoke to her as he would to a child who has just had a nightmare, and it seemed to work a little bit, although she didn't give up her crying. At least the noise was at a tolerable level.

I closed my eyes and tried again. This time the power answered, rising to my call. An icy chill flooded my fingers and spread into the plastic zip ties, freezing them solid. They shattered when I jerked my wrists apart. Yes! Finally, something was going right.

I stood and went to free Olivia first because she was making the most noise. Last thing we needed was to attract the guards to our room to check on us. Although, if she had been whimpering and crying the entire time, maybe they had learned to tune it out. I did the same trick with her zip-ties, careful to freeze only the plastic and not her hands. When she was free, the first thing she did was stand and shriek as she brushed a single roach off her leg. It fell to the ground and scurried into darkness.

I moved behind Ronan to free him. "You didn't happen

to see them with a big black duffel bag full of money, did you?"

"How much was in it?" The plastic zip-tie snapped and he pulled his hands free, rubbing the red ring around his wrists.

I cringed. "A million."

To my surprise, Ronan frowned. "Just one? I would've thought I was worth at least two or three. I *am* a prince. That's practically an insult."

"You were kidnapped and held for nearly a day in an unknown location with a screeching woman, and your biggest worry is that your kidnappers didn't ask for a high enough ransom?" I helped him to his feet. "You're hopeless."

"Kai probably has it, which means we'll have to get it back from him," Ronan said. "But not now. Now, we have to get out of here. Any idea where we are?"

I looked around the room. It was dark, boxy, and mostly empty. There was a single dim lightbulb above our heads. The room had a single door. "I followed the bagman to the sewers where Kai captured me, but I don't think we're there anymore. This feels like a residential building."

"I don't care where we are," said Olivia. "Can we please just leave?"

"Easier said than done." I moved toward the door in case she decided to open it. "There's probably at least one guard in that hallway, and more elsewhere in the building. We'll have to get past all of them, and we're basically unarmed."

Olivia looked me up and down. "But you're a bodyguard. Surely you know how to punch and kick people and so on?"

I stared at her for a moment before I turned to Ronan, eyebrows raised. "This is who you chose to spend your time with? Standards, Ronan."

"Excuse me?" Olivia crossed her arms.

I sighed and put my hand on the door. "Just stay behind me. If anybody comes near you, do what you do best. Scream and flail."

I opened the door. There wasn't a guard on the other side, but I did spy him when I poked my head into the hallway. He was at the other end, walking toward us. When he saw we were free, he paused for a moment as if to verify he'd actually seen us, then broke into an awkward run. After a few steps, he remembered he had a rifle in his hands and stopped to point it at us. I closed the distance in a few steps and pushed the barrel toward the ceiling as he pulled the trigger. The bullets pierced the plaster ceiling, and small white fragments rained down like snow. I wrenched the barrel back toward his face. His trigger finger snapped like a twig, useless. From there, it was easy to pull the gun free and slam the butt of it into the center of his face. He fell to the floor, unconscious.

"Now I'm armed," I said, taking his extra magazines and gesturing for them to follow. "This way!"

My first priority was keeping them safe in the narrow hallway. The second was determining where we were. For that, I needed a window, which I found at the end of the hall. It gave me a view of an unfamiliar rundown residential street. I couldn't tell where we were in relation to the hotel or anywhere familiar, but I was able to determine we were on the second floor of a house. We needed to go down.

Another guard swung around the bottom of the staircase, pointing his gun up at me. It was him or me, so I squeezed the trigger and landed a few shots in his chest. He fell out of the way and I led the two captives down the stairs, sweeping the weapon left to right in case anyone else came running at us.

My military training kicked in. I shouted, "Clear," to let Ronan and Olivia know there weren't more guards waiting to take us down, then waited for them to come down the stairs.

Olivia started to reach for the front door, but I barged ahead of her. It was a good thing, too, because there was a guard waiting on the other side with a handgun pointed at it. He pulled the trigger, and the bullet hit me square in the chest with enough force to push me back. I fell to the floor, blinking away stars and arrow shots of pain in my chest. The bullet had hit me, so it was a good thing I'd put on the body armor. It hadn't penetrated, although I'd have a very colorful bruise there by the end of the day.

The guard didn't see Ronan standing off to the side. He landed a hard punch to the side of the gunman's face, gathering ice on his knuckles as he swung. The punch hit the guard like a truck, laying him out cold.

"Callie!" Ronan dropped to his knees beside me.

"I'm fine," I wheezed out. "Body armor."

He let out a relieved breath. "Oh, thank God."

I sat up with a grunt. "Bet you're glad you bought that upgraded armor like I suggested about now."

"You have no idea." Ronan helped me to my feet. "Are you okay to walk?"

"Yeah. We'd better get out of here before more guards show up." We jogged into the street and turned the corner before I asked, "Any idea where we are?"

Ronan slowed his pace and looked around before shaking his head.

"I know where we are." Olivia pointed in a diagonal line forward. "The hotel is back that way. We should take a cab. It's a long walk."

I patted myself down. "They took everything I had."

"Me too," Ronan verified. "Even my phone is gone."

"Yeah, bad news about your phone. The screen is cracked. I found it under your bed shortly after you went missing."

He sighed. "Great. More bad news. Is there any good news?"

Olivia stopped suddenly and waved to a passing taxi. The cab slowed to a stop in front of us. She opened the back door and leaned in to have a short conversation with the driver before turning back to us. "He'll take us if we want to go. I can pay if we stop by my apartment first."

Ronan and I exchanged glances before he cleared his throat and stepped forward, holding the door open for her. "Olivia, I think it might be best if we split up. Those kidnappers are after me. You'll be safer if you leave on your own."

She frowned. "Oh?"

"Yes, we can always catch up later."

Olivia looked from Ronan to me. "You're not going to

call me later. Let's not pretend." She stood on her tiptoes and planted a kiss on his cheek. "Fate has interrupted us twice now. We're not meant to be. Have a nice life, Ronan."

"You too." He held the door for her until she was in the cab, then swung it closed. It drove off.

CHAPTER FIFTEEN

I scanned the rooftops and empty porches as we walked along, just waiting for Clyde or any of Kai's other people to jump out at us. My clothes reeked of raw sewage and stuck to my body. Slime crusted my clothes that I didn't think would wash off in the water. With time, my nose had adjusted to most of the smell, but every once in a while, I'd get a fresh whiff of it and gag all over again. Ronan walked at arm's length, close enough I could pull him out of danger if needed, but far enough away that the smell was bearable. I didn't blame him. I wished I could walk farther away from me too.

We trudged along, both too exhausted to hold much of a conversation. I considered hailing the next cab we came across but decided against it. The smell was only tolerable because we were in the open air. Cooped up in a vehicle, it'd be unbearable. Since I didn't have any money, I couldn't ask a driver to take us anywhere on faith, and besides, I wasn't yet ready to give up the rifle. We'd be lucky if the cab driver just kicked us out. With as nasty as I smelled and looked and the gun, he'd probably call the authorities to report us. Sane people didn't walk around like this.

Thinking about paying the imaginary driver made me wince. I'd had a million Euros in my hands just hours ago, and lost it. It wasn't my money, it was Ronan's, but that didn't matter. Mab was sure to notice such a large withdrawal. How was I going to explain it when she asked? No doubt she'd chew me out the next time I saw her, and that was without considering I'd let Ronan get kidnapped in the first place.

I imagined her clenching her fists and drawing herself up into a puffed-up version of herself, her pale cheeks reddening with anger as she declared, "A million Euros? How do you lose a million Euros?"

"Mab is going to be pissed," I said as we passed the third white building on the block.

Ronan lifted his head and regarded me with a curious look before it registered what I meant. "You did everything right, Callie. She has no reason to be mad at you. As far as I'm concerned, you went above and beyond what was required of you as a bodyguard. If she starts anything, I'll step in and explain the situation. She can be mad at me if she wants."

"I guess," I grumbled and looked down at my clothes. That was my best jacket, too. "I'm sending you the dry cleaning bill, by the way, and it's going to be astronomical."

"Dry cleaning? I think you'll be better off putting your clothes in a couple of garbage bags and throwing them away. Even the best laundress couldn't get that smell out."

"Yeah, you're probably right." I sighed. "That sucks. I really like these boots and this jacket."

"I'll replace whatever you have to throw away. It happened on the job, so technically, I'm liable for any expenses you incur." He sighed and pressed his lips together as we walked. "Although you're right about one thing. Mab is going to be angry when she finds out about the million Euros. It's not much in the grand scheme of things, but she'll make a big deal out of it."

I raised an eyebrow at him. "Not that much money? What sort of world do you live in where a million Euros is easy money?"

"Fae are basically immortal as long as we stay in touch with Faerie," Ronan explained. "When you live for a long time, it's easy to amass wealth. I haven't been around long enough to build up a huge store, but Mab has. She's ancient. It's why she can support me without any problem, and why she shouldn't complain about doing so. What else is she going to do with all of it? Her wealth just sits there, gathering insane amounts of interest."

"She should use it to do some good in the world." I glanced down the street to where an old man slowly pushed a shopping cart full of cans along. A skinny dog walked beside him, wagging its tail. Times were tough for everyone, it seemed. Everyone but Mab and Ronan.

I considered what I'd do with a fortune the size of Mab's, trying to guess how much it was. Probably a larger number than I could fathom. What difference could that make? She could fund all sorts of charities and relief efforts around the globe, or maybe throw it away fighting a meaningless war with the vampires for no other reason than boredom. Why was it that old powerful people with money were the ones who started wars, but they never had to fight in them?

"She does in her own way," Ronan replied. "She finances people in her court. Start-up ventures, salaries, and homes. The fund isn't endless, though it is sizable, and there are a lot of winter fae who seem to need a little help. Despite appearances and internal squabbling, Mab takes care of her people."

We walked along in silence, stopping at the next street corner to figure out which way to go. Ronan thought the hotel was up one street, over six, and through another intersection, but I could've sworn we needed to turn there. In the end, he was the boss, so I deferred to him.

Ronan tucked his hands into his pockets as we walked. "You shouldn't worry about the money."

I snorted. "I'm not. It's your money. Vaughn said you probably had kidnapping insurance, which I feel like I should know about. Do you?" I looked at him.

He shrugged. "Not as far as I know, but I wouldn't put it past Mab to have a policy like that covering me. I don't handle my own insurance."

"See," I said, stopping and turning to Ronan, "that is exactly what I meant earlier. You don't even know what sorts of insurance you have covering you while you travel. Do you pay any of your own bills? You don't even do your own shopping or your own laundry. How would you survive if you were suddenly cut off from Mab and her court? I'm not sure you could."

"I've never had to." He said it as if it were no big deal.

"No fae who is part of a court should have to take care of everything on their own. That's what the court's for."

"Something tells me if I joined the winter court, Mab wouldn't be writing my rent checks."

Ronan opened his mouth, wrinkled his nose, and snapped his jaw shut before turning away. "No, probably not. But you're not her child, either."

"I've never met an adult man who let his mother pay his bills and tell him what to do with his life. I would never want someone else to take care of me like that. Doesn't that bother you?"

He shrugged. "I never asked her to do all that for me."

"And you never asked her to stop. The more you let her do for you, the more leverage she has to make you do what she wants. If you really want your independence from your mother, you should take control of your life, Ronan. You can't keep living this half-life where you say you hate politics, yet you owe everything you have to a political figure. You're either going to be in debt to your mother and her court all your life, or you're going to have to put your foot down."

He frowned, watching a couple cross the street ahead of us, hand in hand. "Says the woman who can't even choose which court she should belong to."

"This isn't about me." I put a hand on my hip and pointed at him. "We're talking about you. You spent the plane ride here complaining about how lonely you are, yet the only relationships you seek out are meaningless and purposely short-lived. I know you want to blame that on your mother, too, but you're the one letting her ruin your life."

"I can't just tell her to leave me alone, Callie!" He crossed his arms and started walking, this time faster. "If you were part of a court, you'd understand."

I had to rush to catch up. "Maybe. Maybe you just need to set limits and take some responsibility for your actions. Like with Olivia."

"What about Olivia?"

"Oh, come on!" I scoffed. "What did you see in her? All she did was screech and whine. I've met some shallow bimbos in my time, but she really takes the cake!"

To my surprise, he sighed and uncrossed his arms. "On that, we can agree. I never planned on getting to know her or making more of our relationship than a fling. I certainly didn't intend to survive a kidnapping with her. If I'd known we were going to get kidnapped, I would've hooked up with someone more tolerable."

"Or at least someone useful in a fight," I grumbled. "You need someone who can keep you safe if you're going to insist on running off on your own all the time. Especially if you follow my advice and tell Mab to ease off and give you some space."

"Hm. True." He gave a small smile and turned his face to the sky. "If only I knew someone like that. Someone who can hold her own and doesn't mind pulling my ass out of the fire on occasion."

It took me longer than it should have to realize he was slyly pointing out I met both of those qualifications.

I laughed and said, "If Olivia is anything to judge by, I'm so not your type."

"Well, if we're going to base our judgments on our most recent infatuations, then I'm not your type either. You know, it's funny. All the trouble you gave me about Olivia being the security risk, and it's your date who turned out to be the dangerous one."

"I told you—"

He held up a hand. "I know, I know. It wasn't a date. I'm neither blind nor stupid, Callie, even though sometimes I might play the helpless idiot to go get what I want. I can read the look in a woman's eyes when she's interested."

I repeatedly tapped the button to change the crosswalk light. "At this point, I don't think telling me how dangerous he is will change much. I saw him in the sewers." I rubbed the sore spot on my neck, remembering where he'd injected me with the sedative. "Kai has shown his true colors, and he's going to pay for what he did to both of us. You know what I can't figure out? I still don't understand why Kai kidnapped you. He has money. He didn't try to maneuver anything politically as far as I could tell. So why take you? Why the million Euros? What did he want from you?"

"I don't think the kidnapping was about me if I'm honest."

I tilted my head toward him, narrowing my eyes. "What do you mean? Do you think it was about Olivia? What would she have to do with Kai?"

"It's not that." He put his hand on my shoulder, gently turning me so I had to look him in the eye. "You haven't looked at your birth certificate yet, have you?"

I'd honestly forgotten about it. With everything that'd been going on, I had been too busy to look. Glancing at a piece of paper kept getting knocked down my priority list, what with the kidnapping and all. Why would Ronan bring that up in relation to Kai?

I swallowed a strange, sick feeling in my mouth. "No, why?"

"Callie, I think that whole kidnapping situation was supposed to be bait for you, not me."

"Why would Kai need to bait me?" I laughed nervously. "He had a crew, Ronan. At least four people working for him. It seems kind of elaborate to have thrown together in a few hours, and Kai didn't know I existed until the day before yesterday."

"That's where you're wrong," Ronan said, shaking his head. "I think he's known about you much longer than you've known about him. Kai isn't just some random person, and there's a reason you two have almost instantly connected. It's not because of his magnetic personality, Callie. It's because Kai is your brother."

I stared at Ronan. My brother? How could that be true? And how could he know it based on what he found on my birth certificate? Unless…

Unless Kai's mother was someone Ronan knew.

I tried to swallow the dryness in my mouth; my tongue felt like sandpaper. "How can you know that from my birth certificate? It would only say the names of my parents."

Ronan sighed. "Because Kai isn't just the summer knight. He is also the summer prince. Titania is his mother."

I put a hand to my head and wandered forward a few steps. "That would mean…"

"That you are Titania's daughter, and technically, the summer princess."

I staggered, floored by the sudden revelation. There was a reason that it felt like we'd known each other forever, Kai and me. There was a reason we had connected instantly. A reason for everything, except for why he had kidnapped Ronan. How was that even connected? That was just the tip of the iceberg when it came to the questions I had now that I knew the truth.

Not only that, but I had just realized I'd almost dated my own brother. The very idea made me sick, more than the sewage smell of my clothes ever could have. Why hadn't Kai told me the truth?

I put my back against the nearest wall and slid down to sit, wrapping my arms around my knees and pulling them to my chest. "I don't understand. How is that even possible? I should've known. Someone should've told me."

"I tried." Ronan sank to the ground next to me, putting a comforting hand on my back. "Every time I tried to tell you the truth, you shut me down. You said you didn't want to hear it. I should've just told you anyway, but I was so upset about how you reacted to Olivia. I thought at the time it would be better if you learned it on your own. That it would serve you right. I wanted to get back at you. I'm sorry, Callie. I'm so sorry."

He was sorry? Here I was, dazed and confused over the news, and he felt bad, as if it were his fault I had been too stubborn to open the envelope. If I had just looked at it before we left Ohio, how much of this trouble could have been avoided?

I closed my eyes and turned away from Ronan. "I must seem like such an idiot."

"No, you don't." He paused. "Well, maybe a little. But then, you're not the one who got yourself kidnapped, are you? It's embarrassing to think about, really. I will be the talk of court for months to come. 'Did you hear about Ronan?' they'll say. 'The first winter prince to be kidnapped by the summer fae in over a thousand years. How pathetic he is. He can't even protect himself.'"

"Of course, you can't. That's why it's my job."

Ronan snorted. "Believe it or not, I'm not completely helpless. I can defend myself, and I have before. I'm just not very good at it, and I prefer not to."

"What about your magic?" I'd seen him use it, hitting targets in the woods. He had also been teaching me a few things, but those had been limited to basic control and accessing my power.

He shrugged one shoulder. "Like I said, I have my magic, but because I don't spend a lot of time in faerie, it's weakened over the years. Since I almost never use it, it's growing weaker still. Magic is like a muscle, Callie. The more you use it, the better you'll be with it. I've always been much more interested in creating things over destruction. Because I don't have the will to harm other living things, I'll never be good at defending myself. I think that's one thing you failed to realize makes you so special."

"What? That I can beat the crap out of anyone?" I rolled my eyes and shook my head. "That doesn't make me special."

"No," Ronan said, taking my hand. "You can hurt people. I've seen you do it. I've also seen what it does to you when you have to hurt someone. You don't use your strength to harm others when you can help it. You're a protector by nature, and you're a great judge of when to fight and when not to. It's difficult to explain, but keep in mind that I grew up at court. I know what it's like to watch someone powerful hurt someone weak just because they can. You would never do that."

I looked down at his fingers intertwined with mine, my throat suddenly tight for no reason. His hand was warm, inviting, and soft. Those three words were not ones I commonly associated with him or anyone in the winter court. I realized my cheeks were warm and pulled my hand away. "My brother. God, I can't believe it. I just keep thinking about what would've happened if I never found out. How far would he have let it go?"

"I was going to tell you. Even if you didn't want to hear it, I was going to tell you as soon as things cooled off after our argument. I would never have let things go too far between you two."

"Yeah, but how would you know? I mean, he took me out to that bar, and things were going so well..."

"Wait, you two went to a bar? I thought you were just going down to the restaurant in the hotel." Ronan sounded disappointed, maybe even a little jealous. Or was I imagining that?

I shrugged. "Yeah, why not? As far as I knew, he was a decent guy. He was funny, easy-going, good looking—"

"I can be funny."

I crossed my arms and gave him a doubtful lift of my eyebrow. "Really? Tell me a joke. A funny one."

He thought for a minute, rubbing his chin and scratching the back of his neck before he snapped his fingers. "So, two muffins were sitting in an oven. One turns to the other and says, 'Boy, it's hot in here.' The other one turns to the first and exclaims, 'Wow, a talking muffin!'"

I slid my hand into my face and groaned. "I guess I should be thankful you didn't choose to become a comedian. Then I'd have to protect you from all the tomatoes people would throw at you."

Ronan laughed, stood, and offered me a hand up. "Well, what did you expect? It's not like we winter fae have much of a sense of humor. One reason I think you'll fit right in. Just because you were born to summer, it doesn't mean you have to stay there since you haven't declared yet."

He had me there. I put my hand in his, and he helped me to my feet. We started down the street again. "You know, the one thing I can't figure out is why he would need to trap me. Kai had already charmed me into thinking he could do no wrong. Why kidnap you and then lure me out of the hotel like that? Did he say anything, anything at all?"

Ronan shook his head and rubbed his temples. "Honestly? The only thing I can remember anyone saying is what Olivia was screaming about. I've got a splitting headache, and I can't wait to get back to the hotel, get a shower, and sleep off whatever they dosed me with."

"Then it looks like you're in luck." I pointed up the street and to the right, where the Le Bristol Hotel waited.

It took us another twenty minutes to walk the distance and to go around to a side entrance. We didn't want to go through the main entrance and alert Kai that we were back. Also, I reeked of sewage, and I figured as a courtesy to all the other guests, it would be better if we just went up the side stairway. Kai had taken everything from me, including the room key, which I would have to go down to the front desk to have deactivated as soon as possible.

Luckily, Sam was waiting in the suite. As soon as I knocked, they threw open the door and rushed to hug me. It was only after Sam had thrown their arms around me that they took a deep breath and smelled my clothes. They backed away, gagging and pinching their nose. "Were they keeping Ronan in a sewer?" Sam said, waving a hand through the air.

"Sort of. I know I smell bad." I moved past them, headed straight for the shower. "I'm going to need a couple of trash bags to dispose of these clothes. Also, I lost the room key. Could you call down to the front desk and have them deactivate it? Tell them I think someone stole it."

"Wait a minute!" Sam took a step toward me, paused then moved toward Ronan, who was headed toward his own bedroom for a shower. "You guys can't just leave me hanging like this! I need to know what happened!"

"Later!" Ronan and I said at the same time and retreated to our respective bathrooms to get cleaned up.

I took two baths, three if you counted me standing in the tub, peeling off the gross clothes, and dousing myself with water. After that, I got out and had to clean the tub before I could sit in it. The water was still grayish when I got out, so I rinsed the tub a second time and climbed right back in. This time, however, I opened the complimentary bubble bath and dumped it in the water. It made the room smell less like sewage and more like roses growing in sewage. Sam peeked in with a bottle of air freshener and sprayed it around, but that didn't help the smell any. Eventually, I wound up cracking open the window to let in some air.

It was a good two hours before I felt clean enough to get out of the water. My skin was all wrinkly, and the ambient air was chilly compared to the warm water I'd been sitting in. As I was drying off, I spied the manila envelope containing my birth certificate sitting on an end table in my room. Rather than dress, I threw on a robe, grabbed the envelope, and sat at the vanity.

I don't know why I hesitated about opening it. I already knew what it said, if Ronan was to be believed. I had no reason to doubt him, and he had no reason to lie. When I opened the birth certificate, it was going to say Titania was my mother. I had royal blood. Not just any royal blood, either. Summer fae royal blood, which didn't make any sense. The only power that had ever manifested within me was ice. I'd always thought that when I finally found out who my parents were, they would be part of the winter court. I certainly didn't expect the summer queen to be my mother.

What would that mean? What would it change? Would I be expected to attend events like Ronan? To be part of her court? Would I still have a choice? I thought finding out who my parents were would give me answers. Instead, it created more questions.

Still, I had to see it for myself.

Slowly, carefully, I slid my fingers under the flap. I pulled the paper out of the envelope and lifted it so I could read it in the light coming through the window. There it was—Titania's name typed out for all to see. On the line for my father's name, I found "William Hart." Ronan obviously recognized Titania's name, but he hadn't said anything about my father. Who was he? He must've been human, considering I was only half-fae. Did that mean Kai was half-fae too or was he only my half-brother? I didn't know the answers to those questions, and the only way to find out was to ask Kai. He was the last person I wanted to speak to after what Ronan and I had just been through, but I might not have a choice.

I put the birth certificate away, threw on a pair of comfortable sweats and a loose-fitting T-shirt, and walked out into the main part of the suite. I had intended to check on Ronan and to review the schedule rotation for the rest of the day, but I found Ronan standing in front of the large mirror on the wall in the living area, fidgeting with a tie. He had put on his formal suit.

"What's going on?" I asked, hopping onto the sofa.

Sam brought me a cup of hot tea. "Ronan said there's some sort of party downstairs."

"Not a party," Ronan corrected. "It's the formal gala. The main event. I'll be expected to make an appearance, and that's the only reason I'm going."

"Well, Mark and Yvonne are on the detail." I cradled the cup in my hands. There was nothing like a mug of hot tea after trudging through the sewers.

He turned away from the mirror with a slightly crooked tie. "I was hoping you would be my plus one to the event, Callie. Whoever is guarding me, I would feel a lot safer if you were by my side."

I frowned. "Are you sure going is wise after everything that just happened?"

He sighed. "Trust me when I say I don't want to. However, if I don't do something to keep up appearances, it's going to raise suspicions. Then I'll be questioned and have to tell Natalie what's happened, and nobody wants that."

Ronan was right. If he didn't make an appearance, Natalie would send someone up to check on him. The vampires might also see it as a snub, which we couldn't allow. Since this was the main event, Ronan had to be in attendance, and I had to go with him.

I took a long sip from the mug and placed it on the coffee table in front of me. "I'm happy to go with you, Ronan, on one condition. After this gala is over, we pack up our things and leave. No waiting for check-out tomorrow, no waiting for the closing ceremonies. We go tonight. I'm done with Paris, maybe for a lifetime."

"Agreed."

We shook on it, and before we parted so I could dress for the event, I straightened his tie for him.

CHAPTER SEVENTEEN

Since I didn't have the first clue about what to wear to a formal peace gala, I enlisted Sam's help. They had me lay out every clean outfit I had left on the bed, and walked along the line, studying each meticulously, their finger curled around the bump of their chin.

There were two dresses left. My pick was a simple black dress that reached to my knees. I could throw a jacket on over it to add a splash of color.

"But everyone will be wearing black," they said. "If you want to stand out, you should wear something else."

"Who says I want to stand out?" I asked.

Sam picked up the other dress, which wasn't black. It was bright red, and made of the softest fabric I had ever felt. The hem reached the floor, but the top clung tightly to my body and was cut a little lower than I usually wore. It was one of the things Sam had picked out for me to wear when we went shopping and not the sort of thing I would normally put on.

When I tried to make that argument with them,

however, they answered, "Exactly! That's why you should wear it! As far as everyone else there knows, you're just Ronan's human bodyguard. But you're not, are you?"

I crossed my arms and turned away from Sam, peering out the window. "Ronan told you?"

"He didn't tell me what the birth certificate said. Told me I should ask you about that. He did say, though, that it wasn't what you expected. That it made you feel like you needed to be more."

"More what?" I asked, looking over my shoulder at them.

Sam shrugged. "He just said more. I know what that means for you, though. You always feel like you have to earn everything. So tell me what it is. What is it you think you have to earn now?" They eased onto the bed.

"Kai is my brother."

"Your what?" Sam surged off the bed so fast I was worried they would fall over.

"Yeah, and not just that. Kai is also apparently the summer prince. Titania is his mother, which by extension, means—"

"Oh, my God! You're royalty! Should I bow or…?"

"Very funny." I pitched a wadded-up towel at them.

They dodged it easily, ducking to one side. "Seriously, though, Callie! That is good news."

"Is it?" I sat on the loveseat, pulling my knees up and balancing their stuffed owl on my kneecaps. "Now that I know, do I still have a choice about which court to join? And how does it even make sense? All of my powers revolve around ice, right? That and the portals."

Ever since Jax died, I had been trying to recreate the

portals, but even with Ronan's help, I'd been unsuccessful. Maybe it was a fluke power, or maybe it was something I needed more instruction on how to use.

I turned my hands over, studying them. "How does that make me part of the summer court?"

Sam crossed the room and put their arm gently around my shoulder. "It doesn't, Callie. Mab promised you thirty days to make a choice. That means you get to make a choice."

My throat suddenly felt tight. "Why didn't she keep me?" My eyes began to water. "If Titania is my mother and Kai is my brother, why did she send me away? That means my mother has been alive all this time, and she chose to let me grow up the way I did. She could've come to me at any time and rescued me, but chose not to. Why?"

"I don't know, Callie." Sam put their arms around me, and for once, I didn't mind it when they squeezed me so hard it hurt.

"Thanks, Sam," I managed and wiped the tears away with the palm of my hand. "I feel like I have more questions now than ever. Kai is the only one who has answers, but he's the one who kidnapped Ronan. I don't want to talk to him, but I'm going to have to, aren't I?"

"Do you want me to go to the gala with you? I don't have any formal wear with me, but I could wear your black dress."

I shook my head. From the looks of it, Sam was leaning more toward their masculine side than feminine. I knew it would make them uncomfortable to wear a dress, but it warmed my heart to know they were willing. That was what friends were for—to be there for you when no one else was. "No, I think it would be better if you stayed up here and packed our things. I really want to get out of here as soon as this is over."

"Okay." Sam shoved the red dress at me. "But wear the red dress and thank me later."

I took Sam's advice and put it on. I figured the fancy dress would look ridiculous paired with sneakers, so I had to make do with the black heels I'd brought. They wouldn't be as dressy as everyone else's shoes, but I'd ruined my boots in the sewers, as entertaining as it would have been to wear them. Flats were right out.

Sam helped me with my hair and makeup, fussed over my dress, and made some final adjustments to the outfit. While they were doing that, I remembered the diamond necklace Mab had given me and went to get it out of my suitcase. It was the perfect addition to the outfit, and Mab would be pleased I'd thought to wear it. Someone would surely tell her the help was wearing an expensive necklace. Not that I cared what Mab thought, but an ounce of goodwill went a long way with the fae.

When I was as dressed up as I could possibly be, Sam walked me out to the living area. "Ladies, gentlemen, and all others of the court," Sam said with a flourish only they could manage, "your attention, please. I present to you for the first time Her Royal Highness, Princess Callie Hart of the summer fae."

I punched Sam in the arm as I walked by. "Knock it off."

Sam rubbed their upper arm. "What? You are."

Ronan stopped pacing between the chair and the sofa, slowly lowering the hands he'd had folded behind his back. "Callie," he said, sounding stunned. "You look great."

"Thank you," I made an exaggerated curtsy and probably did it wrong. "The credit belongs to Sam."

"No, I mean, you look amazing! It's like you're a different person."

I narrowed my eyes as I rose from the curtsy. "Okay, Ronan. I got it. I'm obviously a swamp monster every other day."

"That's not what I meant." He kept fumbling, trying to explain himself, but with each sentence, he made it worse. Open mouth, insert foot—that was Ronan.

Sam slapped a hand on his shoulder. "Why don't you two go on downstairs? The gala started, like, five minutes ago."

Ronan blinked. "It did?"

I muttered a mild curse and stepped toward the door, but Sam stopped me, shoving a small black clutch into my hand.

"There's a present inside," Sam said. "I was going to wait for your birthday next month, but I figured you might get some use out of it in a tight spot between now and then. I hope you don't need it, but if you do, it's there."

I opened the clutch and found they'd stuffed a sharpened stake inside.

Sam beamed. "It's white oak, the same sort of wood Van Helsing used to stake Dracula. I figure it'll work on your vampires just as well."

"You do know Dracula is fictional, right, Sam?"

"A fictional narrative with some seeds of truth," Ronan added, placing a hand on my lower back. "And let's hope you don't need that tonight. It would be a shame to have to kill vampires during a peace celebration."

We stepped out of the suite and walked down the hall in silence. The carpeted floor ate the sound of our footfalls. After so much noise and conversation, it felt uncomfortable. Uneasy, even.

Ronan pressed his thumb on the elevator call button and stepped back. "You don't like dresses, do you?"

I looked down at the one I was wearing and shrugged. "I don't mind them. Let's just say a ballgown wouldn't be my first choice on an average day."

"And you don't like going out to fancy restaurants either?"

I cringed. "Sorry."

"It's all right." He put his hands in his pockets and bounced on the balls of his feet, waiting for the elevator to arrive. "You should've said something, though. I never wanted to make you uncomfortable, Callie."

"Really? Explain Olivia then."

He choked on a laugh. "Okay, fine. As long as we're being honest, I didn't give a damn about her. Or any of the other women who've come and gone over the last month. I'm tired of meaningless interaction and pointless relationships that never turn into anything."

I stepped forward to press the button again just in case it hadn't worked for Ronan the first time. Where the hell was that elevator? "And here I was under the impression that flings were your thing. Have you ever had a serious relationship?"

"Well," he said, "there is one woman I'm interested in, but she's difficult to read. Every time I try to talk to her to express that interest, she insists on running off to do something else. It's as if she'd rather be more focused on anything but getting close to people."

"Maybe she's been hurt before. People who have been rejected by others sometimes find it difficult to develop new relationships."

"Nah." Ronan shook his head as the elevator car slowed. "I think she's just too stubborn to see it. Any advice about how to get through to her?"

The elevator dinged, and the doors slid open on an empty car. We stepped inside, and Ronan pressed the big B button for the ballroom level.

I leaned against the rear rail with another shrug. "Some people don't get it unless you're direct. You're better off just telling her honestly how you feel rather than trying to impress her."

Ronan frowned. "Impress her?"

"Come on now. I've seen how you are with women, taking them out to the most expensive places in your fancy car and your designer clothes. It's like you don't want them to see you for who you are. No wonder you attract bimbos who are just after your money."

He opened his mouth to respond, blinked, and then closed it quickly to think as the elevator sank. "You know what? You're right."

"Of course, I am."

"Beautiful and smart," he said under his breath. "It's like I won the lottery."

I was about to point out he hadn't won anything when the elevator door opened on a small foyer. Music floated into it from the ballroom beyond, where couples in formal attire mingled with drinks in their hands. It was a little too noisy to have a quiet, intimate conversation, and the elevator was open, ready to dump us into the fray.

Ronan offered me his arm. I took it, and we walked into the gala as if we belonged there. Maybe we did, both of us. I'd always thought this would be more Ronan's world than mine, but now that I knew who I was, maybe it was time for me to get more involved. It would come out eventually that I was Titania's daughter, and when it did, I needed to have more friends than enemies on my side.

I searched the crowd for familiar faces. Natalie was near the front, chatting with several other women, all smiles with her fangs out. Ronan's security was already in place. I spotted Mark and Yvonne moving around the perimeter of the room on opposite sides, just the way I told them. Hotel security trailed each of them, while what I assumed was Natalie's private security hugged pinch points in the room, hovering close in case they were needed.

A small, temporary stage had been erected, and a microphone stand waited there near where a live band played. To call it an orchestra would be too generous, since I thought you needed more than five instruments to be so dubbed. They were all playing orchestral instruments though: a violin, a cello, a clarinet, and a harp, all backed by a single percussionist with a small kit. They played as if compelled, and maybe they had been. I didn't know the extent of Natalie's power, but she had to be pretty high up the food chain if she was running the gala.

I leaned closer to Ronan. "Explain the vampire aristocracy to me. Who's in charge of them?"

Ronan glanced around the room. "Well, it's complicated. They're ruled by a triumvirate. Natalie is one member. Vaughn is another. The third is… Do you see the woman in the black dress with the deep V-neck? Pearl necklace?"

I nodded.

"Her name is Tris. She's the third member of the triumvirate."

"And they're elected?" I asked.

"They are. Every two years. This is Natalie's fourth term, Vaughn's second, and Tris's first. Natalie is a well-known ruthless negotiator. She headed the peace treaty between the fae and the vampires years ago. Vaughn, of course, is a militant through and through."

Someone offered us champagne in delicate glasses, so we took them. "What about Tris?"

"I don't know much about her, honestly. She's well-liked in some circles but despised in others, though why is beyond my grasp."

I studied the vampire from across the room. Unlike everyone else, Tris wasn't smiling or enjoying herself. She had large, worried eyes, the type that had seen death and knew when she was in the room with it. I'd met soldiers like that, but they generally didn't last long. They balked at authority, resisted following orders as much as possible, and left the service the first chance they got. There was a time I would've called them cowards for running away, but looking back, maybe they were the smart ones. One look at Tris told me she was the same sort of person, capable of sniffing out trouble and avoiding it with expert skill.

The crowd parted, and Kai stood on the other side. He and I locked eyes. It was an accident, something I didn't mean to happen but couldn't stop once it began. After a moment of staring at each other, he handed off his drink and started toward us. I had only one option if I wanted to avoid talking to him, and that was to jump into a conversation with someone else. The problem was the only person besides Ronan that I knew nearby was Vaughn.

Better him than Kai, I thought. I did not want to talk to him here. I pulled Ronan over to where Vaughn stood.

"Ah, Miss Hart," Vaughn said, raising his glass as I approached. "I see you've located your wayward employer. Good for you. So glad to see you in one piece, Ronan."

"No thanks to you," Ronan mumbled.

"Actually, Vaughn *did* help," I said. "Sort of."

Ronan frowned, looking from me to Vaughn. "Really? Why?"

"Let's just say I wanted to make sure you didn't miss this evening's festivities." Vaughn's smile widened. "By the way, are you enjoying yourself? I believe this is Miss Hart's first formal outing in mixed company. How is it?"

"It's fine, I guess." I turned my head. Kai was still coming toward us, so I pressed closer to Ronan. "I just wish it was a little less crowded. There are a lot more people here than I thought there would be."

Vaughn bobbed his head. "Yes, the guest list is exclusive, but with everyone bringing a guest, their security, and all the hotel staff, there are more people here than I think anyone anticipated. Not to worry. Everything will still work according to plan."

"And the plan is?"

"Mine," Vaughn said simply. "And mine alone."

"Pardon me."

I had to work to keep from cringing at the sound of Kai's voice.

The summer knight inserted himself into the conversation, barging in between Vaughn and me. "I hate to intrude, but I really need to speak to Callie."

Ronan tightened his arm around mine. "Whatever you have to say to Callie, you can say to me."

"But not to me," Vaughn interjected. "I'm wanted elsewhere. Enjoy your little…" He made vague gestures as if he were searching for the right word, then pressed his lips together, his nose wrinkling as if he'd just eaten a bad pickle. "*Ménage à trois*, I suppose, or whatever it is you fae call it."

"Rude," Ronan ground out, but Vaughn didn't pay him any mind.

Kai swept in to fill Vaughn's space as soon as the vampire was gone. He leaned in and whispered in a low voice, "You two need to get out of here. Now."

"Don't start with me. I know who you are and what you did." I put my hand on his chest and pushed him toward a wall. "I know who I am too. I know everything, Kai."

He shook his head and made no move to defend himself. "You only think you know what happened. You weren't supposed to get hurt. Neither of you was. That was the whole point."

"You have a funny way of not hurting people," I said, rubbing my neck. It still hurt where he had injected me, and my wrists were bruised from the zip-tie.

Kai grabbed my arm and said more forcefully, "Callie, you need to take Ronan and leave. However you feel about me, we can work it out later. Right now, the most important thing is that you two aren't here when this goes down."

"When what goes down?" Ronan asked. "What's going on?"

Kai turned to Ronan, his expression grave. "Vaughn is going to make a move. I don't know who it will be against, but it's going to happen here. Tonight. In this room. That makes everyone here a target. No one is safe."

CHAPTER EIGHTEEN

I blinked, trying to process what I'd just heard. Ronan's kidnapping had never been about the money or political gain. Kai had kidnapped Ronan to make sure neither of us would be at the main event of the peace gala. It was his messed up way of trying to protect me, or so it seemed. That was if he was telling the truth.

I crossed my arms and leaned away from him. "Why should I believe anything you say?"

Kai rubbed his temples and lowered his head. "This would've been easier if everything had gone to plan. As soon as you handed over the money, my man was supposed to escort you straight to Ronan. I was to make an appearance and explain everything. The three of us could've waited this all out in safety. Instead, you had to play the hero, and now all of our lives are at risk."

"Do you have any proof of the claim that you are making?" Ronan asked.

"My information is based on weeks of surveillance data." Kai waved a hand dramatically. "It would take hours to review everything and explain to you how I arrived at this conclusion. By then, Vaughn will have made his move, and it will be too late. If we stay, we could be Vaughn's next victims."

What Kai was saying made a lot of sense. Vaughn had been hinting at something big since the gala began. He had also tried to kill Ronan, and I wouldn't put it past him to try a second time. However, Kai had kidnapped Ronan and tied me up. That made it hard to believe him, especially without any proof.

"It wasn't my choice," Kai said. "After I presented my findings to Titania, she gave me specific orders. All I did was follow them."

"So, your queen ordered you to seduce Callie?" Ronan frowned.

"Seduce?" both Kai and I said at the same time. "Nobody seduced me, Ronan."

Kai adjusted his jacket, clearly uncomfortable with the accusation. "Certainly not. That was never my intention. Callie is my sister. I was just being friendly. Trying to show her a good time. Just thinking about that…" He shivered. "No, thanks. But that has no bearing on the situation right now. I need you to trust me, and we need to get out of here."

"No offense, Kai, but I'm reluctant to go anywhere with you," Ronan said. He took me by the hand. "But I am willing to believe you when you say we are in danger, and I've had enough of this. I'm ready to get back on the plane and go anywhere other than here."

Kai nodded. "As long as you're not here."

The three of us started for the door, moving as quickly

as we could without drawing attention to ourselves. There were three exits from the ballroom, all of which were being guarded by Natalie's security guards.

I pulled back on Ronan's arm as we came close to one of them. "Do you recognize the logo on their sleeves?"

"Vaughn's men," Ronan whispered. "This is bad."

Dammit, how had I not recognized it before? Of course, Vaughn's people would be providing security for the event. Everything should be fine as long as the hotel staff was still around. Surely the hotel would not allow guests to die on the grounds. Yet, as I looked around, I couldn't spot the hotel security or any of their servers. The ones who had been there moments ago had been replaced by people in different uniforms. Meyer Securities uniforms.

Before we could take another step toward the nearest exit, Vaughn's people lined up in front of it, blocking our escape. I guided Ronan away from that door, still doing my best not to make a scene, and walked toward another exit. As I drew closer, however, Vaughn's people blocked that one too. In a matter of seconds, they had all three exits sealed. No one would be leaving.

A smiling server walked up to us and handed us fresh glasses of champagne. "For the toast," she said.

I took Ronan's glass away from him before he could drink it and discarded the contents of both in a nearby plant. "Get ready for a fight," I whispered. "Something bad is about to happen."

Natalie took the podium, tapping her glass with a fork to get everyone's attention. The room stilled, the volume of voices dropping to nothing while the orchestra picked up their instruments and left the stage. Unlike the glasses of champagne that had been given to Ronan and me, hers was dark red.

"Thank you all for coming," Natalie said, managing to smile while she spoke. It was like that stupid smile was glued onto her face.

As Natalie went down the list of people she wanted to thank, right down to the caterers, the bakers, and the custodians, people crowded into the center of the room, everyone but Ronan and me holding a fresh glass of champagne. I searched for Kai, but I couldn't find him. Maybe he'd managed to get out before they'd blocked the doors.

"Without further ado, I would like to introduce my associate," Natalie said. "This man has served vampirekind as a member of the triumvirate for years. He is a warrior, and who better to speak on peace than a man who understands the intricacies of war? I am proud to call him my friend. Here he is: Vaughn Meyer."

Vaughn stepped up to the microphone as Natalie backed away, clapping. He raised a hand, gesturing for everyone to quiet down. "Thank you, Natalie. You make a good point. Only a soldier can truly understand the price of peace. In the time before our long peace, many young men and women on both sides lost their lives in the name of honor and glory. Those are words used frequently by my counterparts, words they acknowledge I understand far better than they. That is why I have been honored to serve as the aristocracy's security advisor for many years.

"In that time, I have seen many powers come and go. Alliances shift, and they are tested, yet, the peace holds. Against all odds, it holds. There are those among us who would argue there is more to gain by going to war, by casting aside the bonds of tradition and the expectation of partnership. It has been my duty these last few years to ensure that doesn't happen, that we work together toward a common good, to better serve the world that we must leave behind for our descendants. It is with that in mind that I ask you to raise your glasses in a toast. For it is more important that our kind look toward the future than dwell on the past. To the future!"

"To the future!" everyone shouted back and raised their glasses before downing the champagne.

The room erupted into applause for Vaughn's speech, and Natalie went back to the microphone, her empty champagne glass in hand. "Thank you for that rousing speech, Vaughn. We can always count on you to lighten the mood."

Several vampires around the room chuckled. Apparently, that was an inside joke.

Natalie cleared her throat. "Now, I hope that you will enjoy the rest of the gala." She turned her head away from the microphone and coughed. "Excuse me. Anyway..." Natalie turned her head away again and erupted into a coughing fit that grew more desperate with time. Another vampire brought her an unfinished glass of champagne, which she downed in a few gulps, but it made no difference. Natalie gripped her throat and went to the floor of the stage, making an awful gurgling sound.

As she went down, several of the other vampires around the room started coughing as well. One by one, every high-ranking vampire in the room gripped their throats and fell over.

Everyone else in the room panicked and searched for

the doors until Vaughn stepped back up to the podium. He moved Natalie's still body aside with a foot and picked up the microphone. "Everyone, please stay calm. This was a targeted attack, and those who were meant to receive the poison have done so. Please enjoy your drinks since they are no more unsafe than usual. You have my word." As if to demonstrate, he raised his glass and chugged the whole thing.

The few vampires left in the crowd surged toward the stage, drawing hidden weapons. Vaughn's men rushed from their positions near the doors to engage.

I grabbed Ronan and pushed through the surging, panicked crowd, trying to fight our way to the exit. We might not have been Vaughn's target, but no vampire would shed a tear for us if we got caught in the crossfire. We had to get out of there. Mark and Yvonne were nowhere in sight. Maybe they had been removed by Meyer Security.

Two vampires were suddenly directly in our path. An aristocrat's guard pointed a gun at Vaughn's mercenary, but he wasn't fast enough. A bullet tore through his neck, and he turned the gun aside in favor of gripping the hole it made. I didn't think a single bullet could kill a vampire, but that didn't mean it didn't hurt. The mercenary who'd fired took advantage and leapt in, sinking fangs into the other vampire's throat. I cringed and turned away, pulling Ronan with me.

In an instant, the mercenary vampire was in front of us, blood dripping down his chin. "I know you." His muscles coiled, ready to spring on us.

Ronan stretched out his hand and a blast of arctic cold

slammed into the vampire, pushing him back. The vampire braced to freeze, but all Ronan's magic could manage was a thin frost. That was enough of a distraction to buy me the time to open the clutch and pull out the stake Sam had made for me. I jammed it into the vampire's chest and didn't stick around to watch him burn. Ronan and I ran for the exit while there was still a clear path.

Two humans reached the door before us and yanked it open. A gunshot echoed through the room, too close for comfort, leaving my ears ringing. Ronan and I doubled over on instinct, putting our hands over our ears. Our hesitation cost us the easy exit; two more of Vaughn's mercenaries jumped in front of it, hissing when anyone came near and waving their guns around.

I searched the perimeter of the room. Every exit I could see was blocked. Blood and chaos reigned everywhere, and screaming people huddled in the middle of the room. They're herding them there, I realized. Vaughn had killed all his vampire rivals with poisoned drinks and trapped the rest of us. No doubt, the humans would become food. What would he do with the fae, I wondered?

"Callie!" Mark hissed.

I turned my head to find him waving at me from behind a column. With no other options, I took Ronan's hand and raced to meet him. Without a word, Mark and Yvonne turned and ran for a set of double doors, the entry to the kitchen. The serving staff had been coming and going through it all night, but somehow the vampires had over-looked securing it.

The kitchen smelled like roasting meat, spices, and dough. Pots of boiling water bubbled and overflowed.

Charred meat hissed in unattended pans. Where had the staff gone? As we passed the walk-in freezer, I shivered, and not because of the cold. A pair of very still legs propped open the door. It seemed the vampires had already secured the hotel staff, or at least the wait staff. I didn't want to think about what it would mean if they'd taken over the whole hotel. My focus had to be on getting Ronan to safety, and the hotel was about as far from safe as we could be.

The guards led us to a back door that spilled into an alley, but I paused just short of going through it.

"What's wrong?" Mark glanced up and down the alley nervously. "They'll be coming. We only have a small window of time to get out, Callie."

I turned to Ronan. "Sam."

He nodded. "We're not leaving them behind."

"How do we get back to the lobby without being seen?" I asked Mark. He'd spent more time going over the hotel floor plan than me.

Mark glanced from me to Ronan and back. "Follow me." He and Yvonne stepped back into the kitchen and let the door swing shut behind them.

CHAPTER NINETEEN

Mark passed me a gun and led us through the maze of a kitchen and out a different exit that took us into Epicure. Just like the kitchen, it was empty, with no sign of what'd happened to the customers. I hoped the restaurant had been closed when the vampires decided to launch their attack.

From Epicure, we slid into the lobby area but halted short of stepping through the doors. Vaughn's vampire guards were everywhere. There were two by the elevators and one next to each stairway. The front desk staff was gone, replaced by a vampire. Another waited by the front doors, which were locked and closed. If we'd been outside Le Bristol when the attack happened as Kai planned, we would've been spared. I guess it really was his sick way of trying to make sure we were safe. He could've just warned us, though.

A fireball sailed through the lobby and slammed into the two vampire mercenaries by the elevators, who erupted in flames. The other mercs shifted their guns, sweeping them in the direction the fireball had come from but not firing. There was a moment where nothing happened, then Kai threw himself at the nearest vampire, driving twin daggers into the vamp's chest with a battle cry. The impact forced the vampire back several steps, allowing Kai to use the vampire's body as a shield while the other mercs opened fire. Once the stabbed vampire began to disintegrate into dust, however, he would be wide open.

I put my hand on the restaurant door to push it open.

Ronan held it shut.

I glared at him. "He may be a jerk, but he's my brother, Ronan."

Ronan slowly removed his hand.

I kicked open the door and pointed my gun at the nearest vampire, unloading. Mark and Yvonne flanked me, shooting at other vampires while Ronan unleashed his magic. The spells weren't strong enough to freeze them in place and shatter them, but Ronan's magic was accurate and effective at slowing and distracting the vampires. Gunfire from another direction forced the mercenaries to split their attention between Kai's attack and ours, giving my brother an opening to take out two more.

Our bullets and magic didn't do much to stop the vampires. I suddenly wished I had more stakes and maybe some made of a non-iron metal. The wooden one I'd used to stake the last vampire probably burned up with him. I didn't know for sure since we'd been in a hurry to get out of there.

A vampire closed in on my right. I pointed my gun at him, and it clicked—empty. He grinned, his fangs gleaming in the light, and leapt for me. The vampire went still in mid-leap and fell face-first to the floor in front of me, one of Kai's daggers sticking out of his back. It shouldn't have been enough to take the vamp down. They had to be enchanted.

I bent over and yanked the knife free as Kai moved to join us. "Mark, Yvonne, get Ronan to the elevator!"

"What about you?" Mark asked.

"We'll clear the way." I eyed the two remaining vampires.

"One for each of us?" Kai said.

We stepped forward while Mark, Yvonne, and Ronan rushed out of the way.

I'd never preferred knives. Don't get me wrong, I'd learned how to use one effectively in the service and as a kid growing up. It was a basic skill that someone along the way had made sure I picked up, and the additional training I'd gotten as a grunt made me deadly with a knife in my hand. Still, I preferred a gun over a knife. Knives were messy and required a lot more skill to use.

Kai's blade was well-balanced and felt right, as if it'd been made for me and not him. If I listened closely, I could almost swear the blade vibrated at a barely audible frequency, growing louder whenever a vampire was near. Yup, enchanted. I almost felt sorry for the vampires. Almost.

Kai went straight for the vampire on the right, closing in to drive the blade into his chest. The vampire batted the knife and Kai's arm away before grabbing his head. I tried to move closer to come to Kai's aid, but my vampire threw a punch that I had to dodge. With his arm fully extended, he was vulnerable. I grabbed the mercenary's arm and pulled his body forward, tipping him off balance and letting him fall right onto my knife.

One vampire down, one to go.

I yanked the knife out as my vampire sparked and lit up, his body quickly consumed and turned to dust. With a quick flip to turn it over in my palm, I twisted. Kai was still grappling with his vampire, his muscles straining as he held the creature's snapping jaws inches from his neck. His arms trembled with the effort. I flung the knife at the vampire. It didn't stick him the way Kai had done earlier; my aim wasn't good enough to do that, but it did hit the vampire with enough force that I got his attention. He snarled at me, providing the opening Kai needed to jam his knife into the vampire's chest. The last vampire fell with a whimper, turning swiftly to dust.

Kai bent over, breathing hard and gripping his knees. "I would've had him without your help."

"Sure, you would've." I picked my knife up from the pile of ash. "We'd better get out of here before someone comes to check on them. We could use another fighter if you're game. In case we run into more trouble."

Kai nodded, but his eyes moved to the elevator and the group in front of it. "Are you sure you want me along after what happened?"

Ronan called, "He's got a point, Callie. Brother or not, he did kidnap us, tie us to chairs, and take my money."

"If you want your money returned, I've got to get back to my room," Kai said.

I extended a hand. "Then it looks like we're going the same way. Might as well go together."

He nodded and shook my hand. We stepped into the

elevator and took it up to our floor first. Rescuing Sam was more important than retrieving the money.

Sam had done as I asked and packed our things. We had to wait for Ronan to throw his clothes into a suitcase, but that didn't take as long as expected.

Kai and I stood outside the suite with the rest of my security team, armed and ready should any vampires come up looking for us. None appeared. Maybe the one good thing about the whole situation was that the fae guests hadn't been targeted.

Vaughn had successfully pulled his coup, though, and the effects of that would echo through the next few months. He had complete control over the vampire aristocracy and could make war without any barriers now that he was their de facto king.

Vaughn Meyer was coming for us. He was just biding his time.

The luggage carts were all down in the lobby, so we had to carry our bags to the elevator and pile them inside. Once we'd done that, all seven of us rode up to Kai's floor —we weren't going to get separated—where he retrieved a single suitcase and a plastic grocery bag bulging with Euros.

He thrust the bag at Ronan. "Sorry about the packaging. The duffel bag she was carrying the cash in fell into the sewage and, well… The money might smell, but it'll spend just fine."

Ronan took the bag, wrinkled his nose, and handed it to me. I gave it to Jim to carry.

Sam was busy rifling through my carry-on.

I frowned. "What are you looking for?"

They looked up. "Huh? Oh, nothing. I was just checking to make sure you grabbed your birth certificate. I don't see it."

Dammit, Sam was right. I'd meant to grab it, but I was so busy guarding the door that I forgot, and they must've forgotten to pack it.

"I'll have to go back for it. The rest of you can escort Ronan downstairs and call the car. I won't be but a minute." I started for the stairs.

"I'll come with you," Mark volunteered. "You shouldn't go alone."

"I can handle myself. Ronan needs you more than me." I waved him off. "Just get him to safety."

Before anyone could protest, I ran for the stairs, taking them two at a time to get to our floor. The birth certificate envelope was exactly where I left it on the vanity. I grabbed it and turned to go, but paused.

A shimmering silver portal waited between me and the door.

"Not again," I growled as it rushed toward me.

<hr>

The sudden shock of white on the other side made me panic. *I'm dead*, I thought. *I'm dead, and this is hell.* But as I blinked, more than the sterile white came into focus.

I stood in a crowded hospital room with a single bed.

Nurses and a doctor crowded around the foot of the raised bed, gently encouraging the woman lying in it. From her red face and position, it was clear I was witnessing a birth.

I moved around the bed, trying to place the woman. She had familiar features, but I didn't know her. I was sure I hadn't seen her before until… The man holding her hand brushed her dark hair out of her face, and I recognized her from the stained glass mural on Mab's throne room ceiling. Titania. Was I witnessing my own birth?

A little unusual, but then, what about my life had been normal since that day at Kloud9?

If that was Titania, then he must be my father. I studied the man holding her hand. He was tall and broad-shouldered with bronzed skin, the color you only got from being outside in the sun a lot. While Titania's features were delicate and soft, his were sharp and harsh, like a man used to working hard. He had the demeanor common in drill sergeants—a no-nonsense, stiff-backed way of standing that didn't match the concern etched onto his face. It was obvious he was used to being able to fight off danger to protect others, an attribute I'd apparently inherited. There was nothing in the room to tell me anything about him, but I knew his name from the birth certificate: William Hart.

I stood on my mother's other side, opposite my father. What a strange thing to say, "mother" and "father." They didn't feel like natural words, but "mom" and "dad" didn't fit either. Those were informal terms used between people who knew each other well, weren't they? Titania had given birth to me, but she wasn't my mom. She'd given me up shortly after I was born. Maybe I'd get to see why if I hung out long enough.

I don't know how long I stood aside and listened to Titania struggle through what sounded like a difficult birth. The doctors offered her medicine to ease the pain, but she refused. William never let go of her hand. He seemed like he cared very much about her and was concerned about me before I was even born. I wished I'd gotten to know him.

I came into the world red and screaming, handed quickly from doctor to nurse to be cleaned up. They took me to a small stand in the corner, where they wiped me down and ran me through the usual quick tests. I expected they'd hand me straight back to my mother, but the doctor never left his position at the foot of the bed, and my mother never stopped whimpering and moaning.

Something is wrong. I was no expert on giving birth, having never done so myself, but this didn't line up with what little I knew. The tensions were still high, and the nurses on alert.

It became clear when the doctor pulled another baby out of Titania, this one smaller, limp and silent.

Kai and I aren't just brother and sister, I thought as the doctor rushed him away to suction his mouth and nose. *We're twins!*

I stood by anxiously as they gently rubbed his chest, but Kai was small, still and blue.

Titania's hand closed tighter around William's, and she sat up a little. "What's wrong?"

Kai coughed and took in a shuddering breath, but he still couldn't get out a cry.

"It's his connection to Faerie." Titania let her head fall back. "I can feel it. His magic is weak."

"Hers is strong," said one of the nurses, holding me up. "Perhaps we can arrange a transfer?"

"It would be dangerous." With his face mask on, I couldn't be sure the doctor was frowning, but his eyes said he was. "And it could sever her connection."

"Meaning?" William demanded.

Titania closed her eyes. "Meaning she will not be able to return to Faerie with us." She swallowed.

"Yes," said the doctor gravely, "but both children will live."

"Then we don't have a choice," Titania said with more strength than before. "They must both survive."

"Callie!" Ronan put a hand on my shoulder, and I was back in the suite.

I choked on my next breath and whirled around to put my arms around him.

He stiffened, then relaxed, brushing his fingers through my hair. "You had another vision, didn't you?"

"Vision, portal. I don't know what they are. It feels like I step into them, then I watch scenes from the past." I let him go. It wasn't like me to hug him, but it'd felt right in the minute. With a grunt and a tug at my dress, I regained my composure, glancing around the room. "Where is everyone?"

"Outside, in the hall, waiting for you." He smiled. "I know you told us to go downstairs, but you took so long, I was worried. I'm glad I came to check on you. Did you find your birth certificate?"

I glanced down at my hands. The envelope was there, so I must have. "Yeah."

"Do you mind if I ask you what the vision was?"

"It was Kai," I said quietly. "I saw… Ronan, Kai is more than just my brother. We're twins."

"Does that change anything?"

"Well, no, but…" I stared at the envelope, turning it over in my hands.

They'd said I wouldn't be able to return to Faerie, that they'd taken my powers to keep Kai alive. That explained why I hadn't known about my magic until recently, but why had that suddenly changed? Why now, and why ice if I was a summer fae? I'd also been able to travel to the winter court in Faerie. Did that mean I couldn't go to summer because of what had happened when we were born? Those were answers only Titania would have, and I would only find out if it were possible if I tried to go there.

"I need to talk to Kai," I said.

Ronan nodded. "But first, let's get out of here. You ready?"

I smiled. "I've been ready to go since we got here."

CHAPTER TWENTY

We left the hotel in a hurry. There were three cars out front, waiting under our people's guard to take us to the airport. No vampires harassed us on the way, although we did spy a few. Whatever they had come there to do, they'd done it. Chasing us would have to wait for another day. Vaughn's focus was on assassinating his rivals for once, not us. While that didn't bode well for the future, I'd take it if it meant we got to live another day.

Kai moved to get into one of the cars with Ronan and Sam, but I grabbed him by the collar and dragged him toward the front car. "Oh, no, you don't. You and I are going to have a talk."

He didn't resist as I pushed him toward the car, only paused to straighten his jacket before climbing in.

"Take good care of Ronan," I shouted to Mark and Yvonne and climbed into the car after Kai.

Despite there being plenty of room in the backseat, it felt crowded sitting next to him. The front car was the smallest of the three, but there was still room between us for at least one other person to sit. Even so, it felt like we were so close we shared body heat, and it left me uncomfortable. I wished we'd taken one of the bigger cars so there would be more room between us.

I folded my arms. "Did you know we are twins?"

"Not until after I arrived here," Kai replied with a casual wave of his hand. "Titania sent a briefing after the fact, along with the order to kidnap Ronan and make sure no harm came to either of you. As I said, I was just following orders."

"Yeah, you keep saying that." I shook my head and watched the city streets of Paris pass. Tall buildings, shops, cafes, and busy sidewalks flew by in a blur, each with their unique charm and character. It wasn't what I'd expected. We couldn't get out of there fast enough for my liking. As far as I was concerned, Paris was an awful city—not because of the people or the places, but because of the memories associated with it. No matter how I tried to look at our trip, I couldn't think of one positive thing to have come out of it. Not only had Ronan been kidnapped, but I'd ruined my favorite jacket, and I didn't get to go on a single tour with Sam. I guess I'd learned I had a family while I was there, but that had nothing to do with the trip. Had I opened the envelope in Ohio, maybe we could've avoided some of the problems we'd had since arriving.

"I need to speak with her," I said without turning away from the window.

"With Titania?" Kai sounded surprised.

I nodded.

He shrugged and shifted in his seat. "Well, of course,

you can, anytime. She did tell me to invite you to tea. It's just…"

"As far as Titania knows, I can't enter Faerie." I turned to study Kai's reaction.

He pressed his lips together and avoided looking at me. Guilty conscience much?

"You knew that much, didn't you?"

Kai sighed and shook his head. "I only know what I was told. They said that when I was born, I was very sickly. Mother had been away from Faerie for some time. Faerie wasn't particularly accepting of fae-human relationships at the time, although that's changed since. Being half-fae is still a mixed bag. Sometimes you're born with a strong connection to Faerie and tremendous powers. Other times, you get nothing. With half-fae blood and no magic, I was left weak, and my survival prospects weren't good. According to the stories I was told, you were the opposite. Born with an abundance of magic. A dangerous amount. More than enough to share with me and still be a force to be reckoned with. They used some sort of procedure to transfer a portion of your power to me, which has kept me alive."

"And that's why I didn't know I had any magic until recently."

"Sort of." Kai made a face.

"What aren't you telling me?" I pinched his arm.

"Ow! That hurts." He rubbed the red spot. "I'm getting to it. I'm trying to remember it all. This isn't a dinner conversation, Callie. I haven't asked about my birth in years. Fae don't generally talk about that sort of thing.

Who has how much magic is akin to asking how much money someone makes. It's not polite conversation."

"Tell me, or I'll pinch you again."

"Okay, okay!" Kai held up his hands defensively. "Titania did something to seal what was left of your powers because they were supposed to be dangerous, especially since the plan was to send you to Earth. Without training, your powers could've spiraled out of control and hurt someone. The story I was told was that they sealed your powers and set you up with a nice family to live out your life, completely unaware of your origins."

"Well, that's a steaming pile of lies if I've ever heard one," I grumbled. "Maybe she meant for that to happen, but it definitely didn't. They put me in the foster system, and I never got adopted. I spent my childhood bouncing from home to home without any sort of stability. When I grew up, I joined the Army and went to war, where I watched vampires decimate my unit. I'm lucky I'm sane after everything I've gone through, Kai."

He frowned. "I'm sure she didn't mean for that to happen to you, Callie. That sounds awful. Our mother is...distant, but not heartless."

I relaxed against the seat. "It could've been worse. I don't mean to complain. I came out decent after everything, and my experiences brought me to where I am today. It hasn't all been bad."

"Life in the summer court hasn't been all champagne and roses either." He leaned on his fist, staring out the tinted window. "Court politics takes its toll. Once I grew up, Titania stopped treating me like a son, and I became her knight. That hasn't been easy, by the way. You know, I grew up envying you and your normal life. You wouldn't believe how many times I threatened to run away and join you as a child."

I laughed. "I probably would've beat you up. I was a rotten kid."

"I wasn't much better. All children are awful to be around, in my opinion." He gave an exaggerated sigh. "The point I was trying to make is that you shouldn't go running to Titania, expecting to suddenly have a perfect life, although the offer to meet is open."

"What if I can't enter?" I'd been able to enter the winter court, but I still didn't know if I could walk into summer.

Kai shrugged. "You have powers when you weren't supposed to. You've also been able to enter winter, according to what I've heard. Who knows? Maybe other things have changed too. Maybe you won't have any trouble walking right into summer. Or maybe you will. There's no way to know except to try it."

"That's what I thought." I sighed and pressed my back against the seat, closing my eyes and rubbing my temples to relieve the building pressure in my skull.

"If you do come to summer," Kai said, "you will have to come alone. Ronan will not be able to accompany you."

I did not see what choice I had. I needed answers, and Titania was the only one who had them. Why had my magic suddenly awakened after being sealed away for most of my life? Why did my powers revolve around ice, not fire like Kai's? What was up with the weird portals showing me the past? Was that something I was doing?

More than that, Titania needed to explain why she had given Kai the order to kidnap Ronan. She also needed to prove to me that she wasn't as crazy as Mab if she wanted me to join her court. Personally, I didn't want to join either court, but if I had been born in summer, maybe that was the way I should go. I needed to know I was doing more than choosing between the lesser of two evils. Growing up without a family and suddenly finding out I'd had one all along had been a bit of a shock. Even more shocking, however, was learning that my mother had ordered my brother to kidnap my employer. It sounded like the plot of a bad action movie, not something that should happen in real life. Hell, everything that had happened to me over the last month didn't feel real, but it was, and I needed to deal with it like the professional I was.

My gut said I needed to know the truth because of the hell I'd been through, but my brain, the professional soldier and bodyguard part, knew I needed to confront Titania about the kidnapping for another reason. She'd risked war with winter, having Kai do what he had. If it was all to save me, then I needed to make it clear that she couldn't pull a stunt like that again, no matter whose court I joined. I intended to make that crystal-clear when we met.

"Okay," I said finally, nodding to Kai. "I'm willing to meet with Titania, but only if you can guarantee I'll be safe."

Kai frowned. "You don't trust me? After all this? Callie, if we wanted something to happen to you, don't you think it would have by now? I mean, you're sitting in a car next to me. Alone. I'm armed."

"So am I," I pointed out. "And I'm better at close-quarters combat than you."

"Do you want to test that theory?" Kai's eyes shone a little brighter.

"Question is, do you?"

He grinned and erupted into a loud belly laugh, slapping his knee. "You and I are more alike than you know! I don't want to fight you, Callie, not today. But I think one day it would be fun, just to see. Today, however, I can promise you this: I won't harm you, and I am Titania's sword. I can't speak for everyone in summer, though, and to guarantee you safe passage is too broad a statement. The best I can do is promise you that I won't hurt you unless my queen orders me to since her order would supersede any promises I made. I don't think she'd order me to harm you, Callie. Not after she had me go through the trouble of saving you."

He had a point, but that didn't mean I had to like it. It wasn't the deal I wanted, but it was what was on the table, and it was better than nothing. If Titania or anyone else tried anything, I could hold my own. I'd fought Mab, and Mab seemed to think I could take her. I liked my odds.

"Fine," I said as the car took the exit for the airport. "Your word that you won't harm me. Just be aware I'll be asking Titania for the same promise as soon as we meet. It's not that I don't trust you. I just don't trust you."

Kai grinned and shook my hand. "Keep your friends close, enemies closer, and family closest of all."

CHAPTER TWENTY-ONE

When we arrived at the airport hangar, Kai and I got out and had to wait for Ronan, Sam, and the other security officers to come meet us. The roars of planes taking off nearby and the engines of our two respective planes warming up meant we had to shout to be heard. Even then, it was difficult to be loud enough. The wind tore my hair out of its neat arrangement and made my dress cling to my legs.

Ronan's hair stood on end. He squinted into the wind as he stopped in front of me. "Everything good?"

"I'm not getting on the plane," I shouted back.

"What?"

I couldn't tell if he hadn't heard me or was just surprised by the announcement. To be on the safe side, I cupped my hands around my mouth and shouted, "I'm not ready to get on the plane yet, Ronan. I'm going to summer with Kai to meet my mother."

He looked at Kai with murder in his eyes, a look that barely seemed to register with my brother. He was too busy leaning against the wall, picking something invisible from under his fingernails. "Are you sure that's a good idea?" Ronan asked. "Can't it wait?"

I shook my head. "I waited to open my birth certificate. I've waited twenty-eight years to meet my family, Ronan. I can get answers now. Today. I'm afraid of what will happen if I wait another day. What if I don't have another chance?"

"Now that's a first," Ronan shouted with a smile. "Callie Hart admitting she's afraid of anything."

He was right. It was rare for me to be afraid, and even rarer that I would admit it, especially to him. I must've been getting soft, but maybe that wasn't such a bad thing. "You see what happens when I take time off, Ronan? Everything falls apart."

"It's just bad timing, you going to Faerie right now by yourself. Who will protect me while you're gone?"

I gestured to the team of security professionals at his back. "I think they've done a fine job so far, and I trust them to keep doing their jobs in my absence. Anyone who screws up has to answer to me when I get back."

Mark suddenly stood up straighter.

"Callie…" Ronan lowered his voice, forcing me to lean in if I wanted to hear what he had to say. He took my hands and squeezed them. "I don't want you to go. I know I've said before that I don't trust Kai, and I know he's your brother, but you've got to listen to me. I feel it in my gut. Something about this isn't right. Please don't go. I'll beg if I have to. I want you here with me."

I cast a look over my shoulder at where Kai waited. He couldn't hear what we were saying, not over the roar of those engines. Hell, I was right next to Ronan, and I'd barely been able to make out what he was saying. There was still time to come up with an excuse to put off the trip if I wanted and take some time to recover from all that'd happened.

But if I waited, I might lose my nerve.

"I'm sorry," I said, shaking my head. "I have to do this. Not just for me, Ronan. Once Mab gets word of everything that happened, she'll have questions. I need to see what summer is like to make my final decision. Kai gave me his word that he wouldn't harm me, and I believe him."

Ronan frowned. "You realize there are a dozen different ways to get around that?"

"Yes, I do, but what other choice do I have? If you go back to Mab without answers, she could do anything. Kidnapping you might be seen as an act of war. Think of my going to summer as an olive branch. I'm trying to settle all this because once Vaughn gets going, summer and winter are going to have to work together if they want to stand a chance against him."

Slowly, he nodded. "I should know better than to try to talk you out of anything. You're a stubborn woman, Callie Hart."

"Think of all the times that's stood you in good stead."

Ronan conceded the point with raised eyebrows and a bob of his head. "Just promise me one thing. Promise me that if anything goes wrong, if you even suspect they might be up to something unsavory, you'll get out of there as fast as you can. You have good instincts, Callie. Listen to them."

I agreed, and he reluctantly let my hands go before turning his attention to Kai. Ronan stared at him for a few moments, as if his brooding glare would be enough to force him to come over. When that didn't work, he walked over to where the summer knight leaned against the wall. Kai looked up and pushed away from the wall with a foot while Ronan gestured to the pilots to cut the engines. We waited for the noise to die down before anyone spoke.

"Did you two come to an agreement?" Kai asked Ronan.

"Let me be very clear," Ronan said firmly, wagging a finger in Kai's face. "If anything happens to Callie, I'm holding you personally responsible."

Kai rolled his eyes. "Please don't threaten me with winter court resources. We both know Mab wouldn't mobilize armies for someone who isn't a member of her court."

"Forget Mab." Ronan drew himself up, standing nose to nose with Kai. "Forget the winter court and its armies. I wouldn't waste my time trying to use them. I'd come for you myself, and I wouldn't hire halfwit idiots to help me. No, that's where you went wrong, Kai. I'd take care of it personally, and there wouldn't be an army that could stop me. If you even think about harming Callie, I will dedicate my life to making sure there is no safe haven for you or anyone you care about. Do we understand each other?"

Kai swallowed. "I think you've made your point."

"Good." Ronan grunted and took a step back.

Kai cleared his throat and lifted his hand from his pocket, holding it out to Ronan. "This seems to have found its way into my pocket. Probably happened during the mix-up." He dropped Ronan's magic ring into its owner's palm.

"A mix-up?" I almost laughed. "Is that what we're calling it?"

"Better that way, at least while we're within earshot of other people." Ronan dropped the ring into his pocket. "I'm willing to downplay what happened to me when I talk to Mab, Kai. Callie will make sure Titania knows that. The last thing either court needs right now is for tensions to ramp up between us. However, summer will have to do its part. No funny business."

"I gave Callie my word, and you made your point clear. Now, if we're done exchanging threats and pleasantries, I'd like to get on with it. I'm sure you'd like to as well so we can all go home and forget any of this ever happened. Callie?" Kai turned to me. "Are you ready to go?"

I turned to Ronan. "Wait for me here?"

He smiled. "Of course."

Sam closed on one side of me. We exchanged a quick hug. "Be good," I told them. "And keep Ronan out of trouble if you can."

"I'll do my best," they said.

Without another word, Kai walked to the center of the hangar, faced away from the aircraft, and slipped on a ring of his own, this one a glowing emerald. He moved his hands in quick circles until sparks appeared in the air. Those sparks caught fire and blazed a brilliant gold before exploding into a burning hole in reality, the other side shrouded in deep shadow.

I lifted a hand near the portal and quickly pulled it back. "It's not going to burn, is it?"

"I hope not," Kai said and gestured to the portal. "Ladies first."

It was the moment of truth—time to find out if I'd be able to enter the summer court or if whatever spell Titania had placed on me as an infant was still in effect. Only part of it might've worn off, allowing some magic to leak through. I'd already considered that might be why I couldn't reliably access my powers. They could still be partially behind whatever seal Titania had put in place. I didn't know what would happen to me if that were true.

Warmth flooded me as I came close to the portal, but it felt less like the unbearable searing heat of a blazing inferno and more like a warm sunny day.

Here goes nothing, I thought and stepped through.

The portal dumped me onto a mound of soft grass populated by yellow wildflowers. Rather than land on my feet, I tumbled through about a foot in the air above the ground and landed face-first. Sun warmed my back as I lay there. Birds sang happily nearby, and I thought I could make out the sound of a stream rushing over rocks.

I pushed myself up as Kai stepped through and gracefully landed on his feet. "Nice trick," I said, dusting grass and yellow flower petals from my dress. "Could've warned me there wouldn't be solid ground on the other side."

"It wasn't on purpose," Kai said. "Sometimes there and here don't line up perfectly is all. When you punch a hole from one world to another, sometimes that means you land a few inches above the ground. Be thankful I'm good enough at opening portals that I didn't accidentally drop you from a mile up. It has happened."

"You?"

He shook his head. "Not me, but someone's done it. Several someones, in fact. It's not always an accident either. Come this way." He started walking down a hill.

When we came through the portal, I didn't realize at

first that we were on the slope of a large hill overlooking a valley full of trees and wildlife. There was no castle anywhere in sight, at least none that I could see, and no sign of civilization.

I ran to catch up with Kai. "Where's the summer palace?"

He turned a full circle, searching the horizon in every direction. "About a mile to the north, I think."

"You *think*?"

"I normally don't come all the way out here on foot, and it's a little disorienting coming through a portal, okay?"

"If you don't travel on foot—" I broke off at the sound of a sharp whinny and turned my head, finding the answer to the question I was about to ask.

Five snow-white horse creatures raced up the hill about a hundred yards away. When they reached the top, they spread feathery wings and soared into the sky, swooping like birds playing in the afternoon sun.

"Oh," I said.

Kai laughed. "You haven't seen anything yet. Come. Titania will be waiting."

A thick grove of trees waited at the bottom of the hill. In the shade, the temperature was ten degrees cooler, but it still wasn't half as cold as the winter court. Small woodland animals scurried along the tree branches. Chipmunks and squirrels made happy chittering noises, while bullfrogs croaked and butterflies flitted through dappled rays of sunshine. In the middle of the grove, I found the brook I'd heard earlier, a thin strip of shallow water, barely deep enough for the few fish swimming among the rocky bottom. The water was so clear it looked like glass.

We came across three deer that went still when they saw us but relaxed when Kai approached. They didn't even flinch when he reached out to pet them, but when I came near, their ears went up, and they bounded away.

I watched them jump over the stream and bounce into the trees. "Please don't tell me you can talk to animals."

"No, not really. But once you've been here a while, they get used to you. I've spent a lot of time in this grove of trees." Kai ran his hands over the rough bark of the nearest tree. "I wanted to talk to you before we went to meet Titania, Callie."

I crossed my arms. "So, that's why you dumped us so far from the castle."

"Technically, we're on the castle's grounds right now. I just thought if you saw everything, maybe you would like it here." He gestured around. "Have you ever breathed air so clean or seen the sun shine so brightly? It gets a little cooler at night, and the fireflies come out. You can hear the bullfrogs sing and the crickets chirp. It really is perfect, Callie."

Based on what little I'd seen of the summer kingdom, I believed him. Everything he'd shown me seemed perfect on the surface, but things with the fae were rarely what they seemed. There was a catch, a seedy underbelly to the perfect world, and I was sure I'd catch a glimpse or two of it before I left.

"You're trying to sway me to choose the summer court."

"Maybe." Kai shrugged and paced around the tree. "Would that be so bad? I mean, you've seen winter. Even without considering the politics and the monarchs, aren't you more at home here? Isn't it more pleasant than the harsh chill of winter?"

"I don't know. I've always kind of been partial to the winter holidays, and I hear the court throws one hell of a winter bash." I plucked a lone daisy from the mossy ground. "It'll take more than a little sunshine and cute animals to convince me to pick one side over the other."

He peeked from behind the tree trunk. "So you're leaning more toward choosing the winter court? Tell me honestly. Is it because of Ronan? You care about him, don't you?"

It was my turn to shrug as I picked the petals off the flower and tossed them into the gentle breeze working its way through the trees. "Maybe. I don't know. He hasn't kidnapped anyone I care about, so those are definite points in his favor."

"And you think the winter knight wouldn't have done the same if Mab had ordered him to do so?"

I shivered, remembering the winter knight's icy demeanor. He would've crushed my skull with his fists if Mab had even suggested it would please her. The winter knight didn't seem human. He never spoke, instead just looming there like the physical manifestation of Mab's madness.

I pulled the last petal off the daisy and tossed it aside. "I have no doubt he would. The point is she hasn't done it."

"But Mab has done awful things too. Look at how she treats her son. Titania would never be so intrusive. In fact, I'm certain she'll embrace you. You could live here with us. And as the summer princess, you'd be a more than suitable consort for someone like Ronan."

I almost choked on my next breath. "First of all, I'm not a princess. I don't care what blood is in my veins. I don't ever want to be called that again. Understand?"

Kai frowned. "But you are. Whether you were raised here or not makes no difference. You are the queen's daughter, and that makes you royalty as much as me. You can dislike it if you want, but you can never change it."

I decided that was an argument he wasn't going to let me win and left it at that. It wasn't the point I wanted to make anyway. "Second," I continued, "why does everyone think Ronan and I are an item? I work for him."

He waved a hand and started walking through the trees again, albeit at a slower pace. "You two argue like an old married couple, and I see the way you look at each other. Ronan was also very upset about the two of us spending time together. I've never been threatened like that by a man who didn't have some sort of romantic interest in the woman he was telling me to keep safe." He stopped to hold a branch aside so I could pass.

"Maybe, but who says I'm interested in him?" I ducked under the branch.

Kai slid under the same branch and let it snap back into place. "You sound awfully defensive for someone who's not. I suppose it doesn't matter, does it? Mab would never approve."

Anger struck me like a hot poker in the chest. "Just so we're clear, I don't give a rat's ass what Mab approves of."

Kai grinned. "I think you and Titania will get along really well."

We broke through the tree line a moment later. The castle lay in the distance, sprawled over two hills with turrets reaching into the clouds. Ivy grew up the stone wall. A huge wooden gate stood open, an arched stone bridge the only way to access it. From as far away as we were, I couldn't count the individual guards moving along the walls, but I could see shapes shifting, scurrying along.

"There it is. The summer palace." Kai hooked his thumbs in his belt loops proudly. "Impressive, isn't it?"

I hadn't seen the winter palace from a distance like that, but I couldn't imagine it looking as beautiful as the summer palace did against the clear blue sky. "It is lovely."

"Come on. I'll introduce you." Kai was already several paces ahead.

I rushed to catch up.

As we came closer, the guards walking along the walls went on alert. I felt dozens of pairs of eyes on me, and probably more than one arrow aimed at my head.

Kai put his hands to his mouth and shouted, "Hello! It's me, and I've brought a guest!"

Someone sounded a horn, and cries of "The summer knight has returned" echoed along the wall.

By the time we made it through the gate, there was a whole crowd of people waiting to greet us. Kai shook a few hands and made small talk with some of the people before asking after Titania.

"She's in the garden," replied a young woman in a blue dress. "Getting ready to take her tea, I believe."

Kai grinned from ear to ear. "Perfect! Then that's where we'll go too."

We walked through the castle courtyard, where people scurried around doing their daily chores. Stable boys carried armfuls of straw, women hauled buckets of water from one building to the next, and the *ting* of a hammer on metal said there was a blacksmith hard at work somewhere nearby. With all the horses being led around or pulling carts—or unicorns, as it turned out—the courtyard should've smelled like a barnyard, but it didn't. A floral scent permeated everything, except for the mouthwatering scent of seared meat wafting out of the kitchens. My stomach growled, reminding me it'd been a while since I'd had a proper meal.

Kai laughed and leaned in to whisper, "Don't worry. Titania always has cookies and sandwiches with her tea."

I didn't think cookies, sandwiches, and tea would be enough to tame my hunger, especially after having smelled what they were cooking for dinner, but I'd take anything.

A large wooden door on the far side of the courtyard opened, and Kai ushered me through into the largest flower garden I'd ever seen. There were shrubberies that'd been trimmed to look like different animals, flowerbeds in the shapes of the sun and moon, and ponds full of brightly colored fish that leapt out when we came near them on the path. Willows and flowering trees leaned in, giving shade to decorative stone benches, and fountains spat cool clean water.

At the center of it all was a huge gazebo where a woman in a bright green dress waited, her back to us. Her golden-brown hair was piled in an intricate series of knots atop her head, each one holding a different-colored flower —the closest she came to wearing a crown.

My heart jumped into my throat as I realized I was looking at the back of Titania's head. I was moments away from meeting my mother, and my feet glued themselves to the path.

She must have heard us coming because she turned her head. Her face was perfect. Deep-brown eyes, a slightly upturned nose, an angular chin... Her smile warmed the air around her. She rose, opening her arms wide. "Welcome, Callie! Welcome to the summer court!"

CHAPTER TWENTY-TWO

I didn't know how to respond. My legs were suddenly wobbly, and my tongue dry as a desert. I couldn't move, couldn't speak, couldn't think. Everything I'd ever wanted to say if I found my mother rushed through my head at once: all the anger over being abandoned, the questions about why and how, the firm demands that she tell me the truth, that she apologize… I wanted to say it all, but couldn't form the words.

All that came out was a tiny choked, "Mom?"

Titania's smile widened, and she tilted her head to one side. "It's been so long since anyone's called me that. I'd almost forgotten what the word sounded like."

One foot slid forward. Part of me wanted to run and embrace her. She was waiting for that, her arms open and welcoming. But I didn't know Titania any more than I knew Mab, maybe even less so. She might've given birth to me, but she'd also ordered what had happened to me in Paris. I needed to know what sort of person I was dealing with before anything else.

I stayed where I was. "Maybe that wouldn't be the case if you hadn't abandoned me on Earth."

Titania dropped her arms, her smile fading. "That was…unfortunate. Please allow me to explain over tea." She gestured to the gazebo.

I considered running. Maybe this was a bad idea. After all, what kind of mother treated their child the way she'd treated me? Yet this was why I'd come—to talk to Titania. I'd traveled too far now to run away just because I was afraid of what I might learn.

I followed Kai and Titania into the little gazebo. It was a simple space with padded stone seats and a large, round table set for three. In addition to the large ceramic teapot in the center of the table, there was also an array of fresh fruits, vegetables, and little cakes to choose from. True to Kai's word, there were also finger sandwiches.

Titania gestured to a fae servant standing nearby, and the young girl came to fill our teacups, passing us each a decorative cup on a matching saucer. The queen picked up another container with a spout and poured milk into her tea. "I assume Kai has related to you the circumstances surrounding your birth?"

"You mean how I had magic, he didn't, and you stole my power to give to him before sealing what was left and severing my connection to Faerie?" I reached for one of the sandwiches. "Yeah, I know about all that."

Titania's frown deepened. "The way you phrased it makes it sound malicious. I promise you, it was never my intention that I choose between my children, Callie. Having twins is dangerous for anyone, but it was especially so for me. I did what I had to in order to ensure you both survived. Had we not siphoned off some of your magic to give to Kai, we would have lost him. It was the only way to save you both."

I took a bite of the sandwich, which had strangely colored ingredients I couldn't identify. Whatever they were, it was a far cry from the bologna and cheese sandwiches I used to eat as a kid. I thought my mouth had died and gone to heaven. It wasn't until I'd eaten the whole thing that I realized Titania was waiting for my response.

I licked my fingers and picked up the teacup, so I'd have something to hold onto. Otherwise, I'd gorge myself on sandwiches. "And sealing what was left of my magic, severing my connection to Faerie? What was that about?"

Titania sighed and set aside her teacup. "That wasn't my intention either. Shortly after the procedure, you began to show signs of a rare and dangerous ability to create rifts in time. Clocks would stop around you. Strange portals would appear, and people would just randomly walk into them. Two nurses disappeared into one and were never found, Callie. Your power was dangerous, and despite siphoning some of it to Kai, it seemed to be growing with every passing day. I had to seal it. Don't you see? Even if you somehow learned to control it, should the wrong people get control of you, it could cause holes in time. People can't be allowed to walk through time portals whenever they want. They might go into the past and change things. They might rewrite all of history and erase us from it." She folded her hands. "The whole universe could've been imbalanced by such a power. I had no choice but to seal your powers and place you as far from Faerie as possible to keep that seal intact. That was why you had to remain on Earth, Callie. It was for the good of everyone."

"I don't understand," I said, putting the teacup back on the saucer, untouched.

"Your power seemed to respond to proximity," Titania explained. "The closer you were to me or your brother, the more frequent the incidents became. Based on the limited data we had, we concluded that being close to anyone of royal blood increased your powers exponentially. When I left you on Earth, I reasoned that it was highly unlikely you would ever run into another fae of royal blood there. The chances were what, less than one in a billion?"

Well, that explained why my powers didn't surface until I was near Ronan. He was the winter prince, and being close to him meant the seal that had once hidden my magic must've cracked, and my power was seeping through. That was why the weird portals were appearing around me, but it didn't explain why my power manifested the way it did.

I glanced at Kai, who stood near the side entrance to the gazebo, leaning lazily against the wall. "I can freeze people solid. I've done it to a few vampires and used ice to hold them in place. When my powers manifested, why did it seem like they were winter powers? I saw Kai throwing fireballs. If his power came from me, shouldn't they be the same?"

Titania shook her head. "Not necessarily. The magic that manifests is mostly influenced by environmental factors. I assume that your proximity to the winter prince influenced your powers, just as Kai's position within the summer court has influenced his." She gestured to Kai. "Winter's power can be…seductive. Dark. Chilling, even."

"Okay, then. Explain what happened in Paris." I crossed my arms, waiting. Her answer to that question would define not only our future relationship but what I'd tell Mab when she found out about what'd happened.

The summer queen sighed, considered her tea, and took a drawn-out sip from the cup before placing it aside again. "When I heard that your powers had manifested, I held out hope that your ability to open portals in time had remained repressed. Once I heard it hadn't, however, I knew I had to take action. For weeks I wrestled with what to do. Then the peace celebration was suddenly looming, and Ronan was on the guest list. I knew he wouldn't come to Paris without his head of security, so I decided that would be the best place to act. It was neutral ground and a city I knew well, having lived there for a time. You, however, were unfamiliar with it, which would make what needed to be done much easier." She folded her hands in her lap. "I ordered Kai to lure you away from the peace celebration to somewhere you wouldn't be disturbed. The best and most reliable way to ensure you would go wherever you were told to go was to stage a kidnapping. Neither you nor Ronan and his...guest were ever in danger."

"So, the whole thing was a setup to get me to go to the church?" My fingers closed around the handle of the teacup, tightening until I heard a snap. I looked down. I'd broken the delicate handle off.

The fae servant rushed forward to take the broken cup, replacing it with another that she quickly refilled.

"I'm afraid so," Titania said. "But the location wasn't important. Our intention was to lure you away from there under the guise of leading you to Ronan. Once there, you would be anesthetized, and Kai would contact me. I would come, replace the seal on your power, erase your memory, and move you to a new location with a new life. It would've been completely painless but for the little prick of a needle."

I almost dropped the replacement teacup. They hadn't planned all that to keep me out of the way during Vaughn's little coup. Was it just a coincidence it'd happened at the same time? It seemed Titania didn't care about what Vaughn had done or about keeping me safe. While part of me wanted to applaud her for being worried about saving the world from my strange powers, I was also disturbed that she thought kidnapping me, sealing my magic, and wiping my memory was the way to handle it.

I set the teacup down with a loud bang. "I figured you were out of touch with reality," I said, standing, "but even you have to realize that sounds insane. That's not the sort of thing any mother should do to her own child!"

"No?" said Titania calmly. "Not even to save the world?"

"You know, you could've asked. If you'd taken the time to explain things, maybe I would've volunteered to let you seal my power again. It's been nothing but trouble to me anyway."

"And you would've abandoned your friends? Your employer? Your entire life?" She gave me a hard look, one that didn't match her easy tone.

I glanced at Kai. "I don't understand. Why would you ask me to do that?"

"Because sealing your power isn't enough, Callie. You'll have to leave Ronan behind forever. Never interact with him or anyone he knows. Us as well." She pushed herself out of the seat and stood, fingers folded neatly in front of her. "You cannot be around fae royalty or the seal will fall apart again, putting us all at risk."

She was right. It would be pointless to seal my power if I was going to continue working for Ronan because he was what had caused the seal to shatter. Not only that, but now I would have to give up the family I'd only just found. Maybe that wasn't such a bad thing, considering Kai and Titania both seemed like they were nuts.

Kai stretched and stood up straight. Titania slid around the table toward me.

I moved away from both of them. "You could've just asked. That's what normal people do, you know."

"If we had asked, you would have agreed?" Titania took another step toward me.

I eyed the only other exit from the gazebo. "Maybe. Maybe not."

"Well, now is your chance to decide," she said. "Now that you're here, we can complete the procedure with your consent."

I gazed at Titania. If what she was saying was true, what choice did I have? Punching holes in time and screwing up the balance of the universe didn't sound like a good thing. Certainly not something I wanted to do. I wanted to help and protect people, not cause strange disappearances and weird holes in time.

But if I went along with what Titania wanted, she'd also erase my memory. I'd not only forget about her and Kai but Ronan and Sam too. To me, it'd be like they never existed, and she could make me believe whatever truth she wanted about my life. Just because I forgot about Sam and Ronan, though, it didn't mean they'd forget about me. Sam especially would never give up looking for me if I didn't come back. I'd promised Ronan I'd return safely, that I'd get out of there if anything even felt wrong. This definitely felt wrong.

"There has to be another way," I said.

"There is no other way." Titania put one hand on the table and dragged it along as she tried to close on me. "This is the only spell that will work on someone as powerful as you are, Callie. Don't you think I wracked my brain when I first heard I would have to give up my only daughter? Don't you think I tried to find something, *anything* else that would work? I had all of the summer court working on another solution, but there isn't one. This is all there is. Our only choice. I'm sorry. No one should ever have to make the choice to give up their life and their memories. I don't wish it upon you, child. But I see no other way."

I slid out from behind the stone table and backed toward the secondary exit. "I think I'd like to go. Maybe think it over for a day or two and then get back to you."

"Unfortunately, I can't allow that. The longer you're out there, the more dangerous you become." Titania snapped her fingers.

Kai was suddenly a blur of movement. He appeared behind me, one hand on my shoulder, preventing me from fleeing.

I pulled my shoulder away, turned on him, and punched him in the face. "You promised!"

He pulled his hand away from his lip streaked with red and looked at Titania. "I'm sorry, Callie. I promised I wouldn't harm you, but I didn't promise I wouldn't restrain you. This is for the best."

"Take her!" Titania shouted.

I tried to shove past Kai and run for the exit, even though I didn't know where I would go. The whole castle would be on guard at a word from the queen, and I didn't know how to get home from there anyway.

"I'm sorry," Kai said again and grabbed my shoulders.

CHAPTER TWENTY-THREE

I tried to wriggle away, to shrug my shoulders, twist and punch him. Somehow, he'd gotten too good a grip, and I couldn't get free. In one firm motion, Kai spun me to face Titania and held me against him so I couldn't escape. I threw my head backward to make contact with his nose, but couldn't get enough force in the strike at the weird angle.

"You lying son of a bitch!" I snapped my teeth at his arm, but he pulled away in time.

Kai drew a sharp breath, more harmed by the insult than the physical jabs. "It's for the best," he muttered. "I'm sorry, Callie. It's not up to me."

Titania closed, her hands outstretched, fingers curled as if she were holding an invisible ball. Her lips moved as if she were chanting a spell, but I didn't hear her saying anything. Wind whipped through the gazebo, knocking over cakes and pushing ceramic plates to the stone floor, where they shattered. The tea kettle scooted to the edge of the table and teetered there for a moment, then crashed to the floor, spilling dark tea over the sharp edges of the smashed tea set.

"I'm your *daughter!*" I shouted to be heard over the wind. "I've only just discovered that, and you want to erase it from my memory?"

Titania blinked, and a tear raced down her cheek. "I don't want to, child, but you've left me no choice."

"I can control it," I said, still trying to twist free of Kai's grasp. "I've been learning, and we can get another teacher. A better teacher."

Titania shook her head. "I won't take that risk. You could lose control at any moment without warning and destroy us all. I'm sorry you've had to carry this burden, Callie. This is the only way I know of to fix things. Had I known…" She shook her head. "Perhaps I would've taken more of your power when you were a baby."

"Then take it now," I stopped fighting Kai. "Take all of it if you want. I don't need magic, but I do need my memories."

"Think about it, Callie," Kai said. "Weren't you just complaining about the difficult life you had? All the things that happened to you when you were growing up, your memories of war, all the fights you've had with Ronan, killing your friend… That can all go away. It'll be like none of that ever happened. You can have a new life, a good life. You can be happy."

I considered the offer, despite my initial knee-jerk reaction that it was a bad thing. Maybe it wasn't. If I had my power sealed and my memory erased, I wouldn't even know, would I? And didn't most of the misery in my life come from remembering how awful things used to be? What if that were suddenly gone? For the last month, all I'd wanted was for things to go back to normal. Well, here was my chance. The offer to fix everything was staring me right in the face.

No, I thought. Not everything. A memory wipe would take away all the bad, sure, but with it would go all the good memories. I'd forget about the day I met Sam. They had been more like family to me than anyone, and after their family took a step back, I was all they had most of the time. We'd celebrated holidays together, gone on vacation together, done everything together.

And then there was Ronan. We hadn't known each other for long, but the month we'd had felt like a lifetime. Sometimes, that was a bad thing. We argued about small details, about his decisions and the way he didn't seem to care about his own safety. That didn't keep me from caring about him, maybe even more than I was ready to admit out loud. I'd forget his laugh and the way he'd absently tap his fingers on the backs of the books he was reading. It used to drive me crazy, but in a strange way, it was also endearing. I'd forget the long walks we took in the woods to talk about magic and the way the fae courts worked right alongside the strange, gut-churning feeling of betrayal I'd felt when he took Olivia out for lunch.

Was I ready to throw all those memories away?

Yet if I didn't, my powers could be a danger to others. Titania was right about one thing; there wasn't anyone out there who knew how to teach me. At least not anyone Ronan or I had found, and we'd been scouring the records. And didn't my *mother* care that she was altering my life yet again? Surely now that she'd met me, I was at least a little important.

"You don't know for certain," I said after considering it again. "You can't know for sure that I'll lose control."

"No." Titania's tone was grave, apologetic. "You're right. I don't know, but I know the odds. I know that the last time powers such as yours surfaced among our kind, we had to go to war to stop the person wielding them. I don't want to do that again. I know you don't either, Callie."

"Stop being selfish," Kai snapped at me. "You're one person, and you're getting a better life out of it. The world is at stake. A few shitty memories aren't worth it, are they?"

His words sparked a new fire in my chest. I turned my head. "Those shitty memories have made me who I am. You want to take that away from me, not because you want to save the world, but because you're afraid of what I'll become. You don't know me. That's more evident with every word that comes out of your mouth. If you did, you'd know I'd die before I let anything happen to the people I care about. I don't need you to preemptively seal my power because you think I can't handle it, or that maybe one day I'll lose control. You don't even know the odds, do you?"

Titania turned away.

"That's what I thought. For all you know, you could be erasing my memory and destroying the life I've chosen for no good reason."

"That's the problem!" Titania balled her hands into fists. "We *don't* know, Callie, so we must take extreme measures to prevent the possibility that you aren't the exception to the rule. You have been among humans for too long and adopted their selfish ways. Your memories, your experiences, and even your life mean nothing here. Only my will matters, and you will obey!"

I turned my head to look at Kai over my shoulder. "This is the woman you choose to serve? She's a dictator!"

"She is my queen," Kai said almost apologetically. "I cannot disobey her."

"If that's what it means to be part of a fae court, sacrificing my free will and living at the whim of a madwoman, then pardon my French, but fuck this shit. I'm out." I threw my head back hard.

Kai had relaxed his grip on me since I stopped fighting, a mistake he felt when the back of my head cracked against the bridge of his nose. On instinct, he let go of me and reached to cover his injury. I pushed him out of the way and ran for the garden exit. Behind me, Titania screamed for her guards to stop me. Armor clanked as they moved into position, blocking the exit. I lowered my body and tucked my head, bracing for impact. All I had to do was break through their line...and then what? I'd have to keep running until I found a way out of Faerie, or until someone came looking for me, but I could worry about that once I made it past the guards.

"Gotcha!" Hands wrapped around my leg and pulled my feet out from under me.

I hit the ground chin-first and bounced, rolling onto my back just in time to raise my hands in front of my face. It was the only thing that kept Kai's fist from connecting. When he drew his hand back, I saw I'd bloodied his nose with the headbutt, maybe even broken it. I felt a stab of pride. So much for his good looks.

He fumbled to move my hands aside and managed to

land a punch to my ribs while I kicked him in the side of the knee. I got in a weak punch to his side with my left fist, barely enough to register. The second one in the same spot did, though, and he lost his balance, holding himself atop me by putting his fist into the dirt. Kai came back with a handful of grass and dirt that he threw into my face.

I had just finished spitting out the clod of dirt that went into my mouth when I looked up to see him pause with a fist raised. Light flashed across his face. I tipped my head to see what was happening. Someone had opened a portal, through which stepped the winter knight, Sam, and then Ronan.

The winter knight drew his sword and pointed it at Kai.

"Step away from her," Ronan ordered, "or die."

Kai gritted his teeth but stood just the same.

"You have no claim here." Titania stormed over to stand by her son's side. "Callie is not a member of your court. She's not a member of any court! You can't just come in here, threaten my knight, and demand that we give her to you, Ronan. I don't care who you are."

"We have every right to be here." Sam offered me their hand. "Callie is our friend, and you're holding her against her will."

I took Sam's hand and stood, brushing dirt and grass from my dress. They handed me a gun. I checked to make sure it was loaded and the safety was off before pointing it at Kai. "I'm walking out of here, and you're going to leave me alone whether you like it or not."

"If you try to stop us," Ronan added, "I will consider it an act of war."

"What would your mother say to that?" Titania scoffed.

Ronan smiled that cold, dark smile. "She's not here. I am. If you want to argue with her about it, I suggest you let me leave. Otherwise, you will be speaking to her, and I promise you I'm far more reasonable than Mab will be. As Callie said, we'll be leaving. If I even think one of you might be following us or causing her any trouble whatsoever, you'll regret the day you crossed her."

Titania drew herself up, her face growing redder with each syllable. "You don't know what you're doing! Her power is dangerous!"

"Then I'll find a way to deal with it," I said. "But you don't have the right to decide how. What happens to me is my choice. You gave up any say in that the day you chose to leave me on Earth."

Titania's face suddenly softened. "Callie, please. I meant well."

"Then prove it."

Titania looked around the garden as if she were seeing all her armed guards and Kai's bloody nose for the first time. With a heavy sigh and a wave of her hand, she ordered her people to lower their weapons.

I pointed my gun at the ground but didn't take my finger off the trigger.

"Very well," Titania said quietly. "Return to your life. Do as you wish. But there are consequences to that decision, Callie. I cannot allow you to join my court if you will not abide by my rules."

I grunted. "Good. I wasn't really into the whole summer court thing anyway."

"Just one thing." Titania took another step forward as I turned to go. "If you feel your control begin to slip—and someday it will—my offer to seal your power remains open."

Ronan's hand closed around mine. "Come on, Callie. Let's get out of here."

I turned my back on the summer queen, on my mother and my brother. I had all the family I needed.

CHAPTER TWENTY-FOUR

We stepped through the portal and found ourselves back in the airplane hangar. Although the winter knight hadn't been there with us when we went in, he was there now, staring at me from behind his eyeless mask.

I took an uneasy step away from him. "How did you know to come find me?"

Ronan shrugged. "I told you Kai and the summer fae were dangerous and not to be trusted. Good thing I'm almost as paranoid as you."

"Thanks for saving me anyway." I punched him lightly in the shoulder. "Although I had most of the hard work done by the time you and the cavalry arrived."

"True," Ronan said, rubbing his shoulder. "Guess that makes us even?"

I grunted and laughed. "Not even close."

The winter knight was suddenly in front of us. I hadn't seen him move, but he was there, looming over us.

I cleared my throat. "You have my gratitude as well, Sir

Knight." It sounded silly, but that was how I'd heard the fae speak to one another.

The winter knight said nothing, of course.

Ronan nodded and walked away to make another portal, this one to winter, to take the knight home. The winter knight cast me one last long look before he left.

I shivered and rubbed my shoulders. "Why did you get him?"

"Legitimacy," Ronan said. "If only Sam and I showed up, my threats would've had no weight. I had to call in my one and only favor with the knight to get him to make an appearance, and he only came because Mab was taking a nap. She has no idea any of this happened. I'd like to keep it that way."

"Won't she find out?" Sam asked.

Ronan started for the plane. The cars were gone, so the luggage must've already been brought aboard. "Some of it, yes. She'll eventually find out that I was kidnapped and rescued, but to save face, summer won't come forward with that information. Aside from Kai and Titania, we're the only ones who know the truth, and I'm not going to tell her. Are you?"

"Not if I can help it," I said.

Sam agreed with a nod. "Me neither."

We settled into the cabin as the engines warmed up for all the pre-flight checks. I sat with Ronan while Sam went back to hang out with the security team. They didn't say they were giving us space to work things out, but it was pretty obvious that was what was going on. Unfortunately, I had other things on my mind. All Titania's talk about my powers had me worried. We'd solved the immediate issue and freed me, but I had to make sure I controlled my powers, especially now that I knew how dangerous they could be.

"What's wrong?" Ronan asked, buckling in.

"Titania was right."

"Oh?"

"About my powers," I explained. "I can't control those portals in time. I don't know how. I can barely get any of my powers to respond, and that's after you and I have been working on it together for a month. What if she's right about the other part too? What if I do lose control, and someone gets hurt?"

"You won't," Ronan promised, taking my hand. "There's still the person who taught me, and there are other teachers out there, I'm sure. While we haven't been able to find one who possesses the same powers as you, I'm sure they exist. We just need to spend more time tracking them down is all. I promise I'll dedicate all my free time to it."

"All work and no play makes Ronan a dull boy," I said with a smile. "Now who doesn't know how to relax?"

"You're right. Maybe only eighty percent of my free time." He pulled his hand away and my palm suddenly felt uncomfortably cool, as if the only thing that'd been keeping me warm was holding onto him. "For what it's worth," Ronan continued, "I think we should start with the people I know. If we can't find a single person to train you and help you master your powers, perhaps a combination of approaches would be best. Maybe if they all work together, we can find something that helps you. But it's up to you. What do you want to do?"

"First, I want to go home and crawl under the warmest

blanket I have," I said. "Then I'm going to order a pizza and binge-stream something on the TV until I pass out. My plan is to sleep for exactly eighteen hours, then wake up and take the longest bath in the world."

"Eighteen hours, huh?" He rubbed his chin. "I suppose that means I should give you a couple days off, just to be safe."

"I think so."

"What about Vaughn?"

Vaughn. I had hoped it'd be a few more hours before I had to think about that devious vampire and what he was up to. In one move, he'd eliminated his competition and taken over as head of all the vampires in the world. Even more disturbing, he'd done it right under our noses and almost gotten both fae courts caught in the crosshairs. If he'd been a little more thorough, he would've killed all of us, and the fae and vampires would already be at war.

I crossed my arms, more because of the cold than anything. "War is coming. That's inevitable now. We need to be prepared. Over the next few days, we need to meet with Mab and encourage her to build up her forces and step up security. Whatever she needs to do to be ready. The same is true for you. We'll need a few more bodies if we want to run a tight security schedule. That means hiring two or three more people. Are you good with that?"

Ronan nodded. "I think that would be best, and I trust you to fully vet any candidates."

The plane rumbled, and the seatbelt light came on.

"Good," I said, buckling up. "In the meantime, keep your doors locked, and don't invite anyone over I haven't cleared. I mean it, Ronan."

He smiled and leaned on his fist, giving me a strange look. "I wouldn't dream of it."

The plane landed in Columbus just before ten p.m. local time. As usual, I made sure Ronan got home safely. We were exhausted as we hauled his luggage through the door and ready to call it a night. Unfortunately, Mab had other plans. She was waiting for us in the living room.

She swept past me with a swirl of cold air and took Ronan's chin in her hands. "Let me look at you. Well, you look no worse for wear. At least you've come back in one piece."

"I take it you heard what happened." He dropped his suitcase to the floor with a loud bang.

Mab withdrew her hand. "Which part are you referring to specifically, my son? Your kidnapping, or the vampire coup? Either could've claimed your life."

"But neither did, thanks to Callie." Ronan put an arm around me and pulled me closer.

Mab narrowed her eyes. "Yes, I see. I don't mean to push, child, but the deadline is fast approaching. You've seen what summer has to offer by now, no doubt. I know their liaison was in attendance. Have you come to any conclusions?"

I took a step away from Ronan. "Did you know? About my parents and Kai, I mean?"

"I suspected." Mab folded her hands in front of her. "Sometimes twins are born with opposite tendencies. It would make sense that your brother's powers manifested as part of summer and yours leaned more toward winter. Or it could simply be that you've been exposed to my court more and adopted some of our ways unconsciously. Either way, you clearly fit in better with the winter fae. Do you not agree?"

I glanced at Ronan, who nodded. He had my back, whatever I chose. "I've seen the power that both the winter and the summer queens have. How each of you runs your court. You both ask for blind loyalty from your subjects, which I suppose is your right as queen. But you rule like despots. You order people around just because you can and constantly thrust yourselves into other people's lives in order to control them. Anything you can't manipulate or control, you hate."

"I never—"

I cut the queen off. "I'm not finished. Maybe the other fae are used to it. Maybe that's how it's always been. I don't know, and I don't think that's a war I can win. I can't change how you choose to run things, but I don't have to be a part of it. I don't want anything to do with either court. I'm going to remain independent."

Mab's eyes widened. "You can't! I won't allow it!"

"You don't have a choice." I crossed my arms. "You can't force me to join your court any more than Titania can force me to join hers. You could try, but it'll cost you more than it's worth. I've defended myself against both of you and kept Ronan safe. I can more than hold my own against anyone who wants to challenge me. If anyone should have the right not to choose, it's me."

"But there's a war coming!" Mab ground her heel into the floor. "Without a court, you'll be alone. Vulnerable.

They will come for you first, and there will be no safe haven for you in summer or winter."

"I've gone up against Vaughn before," I said. "He can try to take me out. He'll fail. And I don't need summer's or winter's protection. I've proven that already by surviving on my own as long as I have."

Mab turned to her son. "Ronan! Talk some sense into her!"

He tilted his head to the ceiling and laughed. "If I could do that, don't you think I would've? You have a better chance of convincing a lion to have tea with you than convincing Callie she's wrong. Honestly, she's not, though. Callie is the most capable woman I know. After all she's done for me, I'm happy to support whatever she wants to do."

"Thank you," I said to Ronan.

Mab stomped her foot again. "This is madness! You'll be dead within the week!"

"Maybe. Then again, maybe not."

The winter queen took a deep breath, eyes widening as she tried to calm the raging storm within. It took her more than a few moments to compose herself, but she managed it eventually with the help of more deep breaths. "Very well, Callie Hart. If that is what you want, far be it from me to try to convince you otherwise. But know this. You cannot change your mind. When they come for you—and they will—you will regret your decision. Mark my words, child!" She turned to Ronan. "I expect you'll make a full report tomorrow. Until then, goodbye and goodnight!" She marched out of the house, her head held high.

I sighed. "She really does live in her own little world, doesn't she?"

"Must be lonely in there," Ronan said. He walked over and shook Sam awake from where they'd curled up like a cat on another suitcase near the door. "I think you'd better take Sam home, Callie. It's been a long day for all of us."

"I'm fine." Sam stood and yawned. "I can drive."

"I'm driving," I said and went to the door. "When do you want me back?"

He looked around him, his face falling as he realized he'd be spending the night alone in his house with just the guard on duty for company. "As soon as you're willing to come," he answered.

I nodded. "Day after tomorrow it is then."

Sam was asleep in the car when we pulled up to the loft, but the nap seemed to do them good. They were wide awake by the time I unlocked the door, which was just fine with me. They could carry the luggage inside while I found us something to eat.

"Why don't we go out?" Sam said, tossing one of their garment bags onto the back of the sofa.

I frowned into the empty fridge. "Might have to. There's nothing to speak of in here, but I don't know if I want to go to a fast food place, and those would be the only restaurants open this late."

"I could go to the store and grab a few things?" Sam offered.

I closed the fridge and turned around, putting my back

to it with my arms crossed. This was the first time Sam and I had been alone since I overheard their conversation with Ronan earlier. I'd always thought Sam had my back—that they were on my side no matter what, but especially when it came to men. It'd always been me and Sam against the world. To hear them complaining about me right along with Ronan kind of hurt, and it needed to be addressed so I could make sure things were still good between us.

"Sam, I overheard what you and Ronan were saying about me in the suite. About how you agreed with him that I was being unreasonable and too restrictive."

"Oh." Sam plopped down on the loveseat, cringing. "You heard all that?"

I nodded and slid onto a stool at the counter. "Whatever happened to sisters before misters, huh?"

Sam sighed and rubbed the back of their neck. "That's the thing, isn't it? I'm not always a sister. Look, the thing is, sometimes it's easier for me to sympathize with Ronan. I don't know. We just click. Not romantically or anything, but when I'm having a dude day, we're bros."

"So, it's bros before hos now, huh?"

Sam snorted. "Well, I don't know about that. Guys like to bitch and moan as much as chicks do. I guess sometimes I just need another outlet with someone who understands that stuff, you know?"

"Great," I said, putting my head in my hands. "So, what you're saying now is that between you, me, and Ronan, there are basically four people in three bodies?"

Sam shrugged. "My friendship with Ronan is different from my friendship with you. We can still be like sisters.

I'm still on your side, Callie…for about two weeks out of every month."

"Well then," I said, "I reserve the right to bitch about Ronan as much as possible during those two weeks, and you have to listen to me."

"Deal." Sam laughed.

We hugged, and they agreed to run to the store to pick up enough food to get us through the next twenty-four hours.

While they were gone, I jumped in the shower. My plan was to crash after Sam brought food back, but they hadn't come home yet, so I went straight to the computer. The envelope containing my birth certificate was sitting next to it. I must've put it there as soon as I came through the door.

My trip to Paris had told me everything I needed to know about my brother Kai and my mother Titania, but I still knew next to nothing about my father. All I had was a name, and I could run a search with it.

I found a genealogy website and was in the process of putting in the name William Hart when there was a knock on the door. I froze. Sam wouldn't knock. They'd taken their key. No one else would knock on the door, at least no one I was expecting. Just to be on the safe side, I took my gun to the front door while I peered through the peephole.

Ronan was on the other side, holding two pizza boxes. He looked like he'd showered too, and changed out of his formal clothes, exchanging them for a pair of jeans and a plain t-shirt. I wouldn't have thought he even owned jeans.

With a sigh, I put the gun aside and opened the door. "What are you doing here? And where is your guard?"

"I came to apologize for what happened in Paris, and I brought gifts. And David came with me to this floor and waited at the elevator. I told him to leave if you opened the door. You can yell at him later." He held up the boxes.

I frowned, knowing exactly how he felt about my choice of pizza toppings. And I would be discussing our procedures with the team *yet again*. But as he lowered the boxes, I spied what was on top: a brand new copy of *Die Hard* on DVD, still in the shrink wrap. *"Die Hard?"*

Ronan shrugged. "I've never seen it, but I remembered you saying you liked it. The bottom pizza is no sauce, all cheese and crust, just the way you like it." He leaned in. "It's also very hot and burning my hand, so I'd like to put it down."

He's doing what I asked, I thought. *Meeting me halfway. How am I going to say no to that?* I laughed and stepped aside, inviting him in. Like hell, I was going to say no to my favorite pizza with one of my favorite people. "I'll never turn away the chance to watch a Bruce Willis movie."

"You sure you don't have some work to do?" He slid the pizzas onto the counter and turned around. "I don't want to interrupt."

"Nah," I said, closing the door and locking it. "I think I'll take the night off."

If you enjoyed this adventure with Callie Hart, you may also enjoy Bailey Nordin's story in the WereWitch series, also from Renée Jaggér.

If Were tradition forced you to marry at twenty-five, would you do it?

Bailey Nordin is feeling the stress of pack obligations arriving too soon in her life.

She prefers working on cars to going on a date.

A good fight is just a morning's workout, and Bailey's sarcastic wit has killed any chance of a love life.

Her future isn't looking bright.

Roland is on the run from three powerful witches who want him for...*what he can provide.*

Trying to hide from the witches, he ends up in the middle of a town so small, it's hard to find it on a map.

She's a Were, He's a wizard. He could be her ticket out of her problems—if she believed in magic.

Massive changes are coming down from the heavens, and Bailey Nordin is the Were in the middle.

Will she figure out how to break from tradition?

"It's like Romeo and Juliet... A Were and a wizard fighting kidnappers, gods, and a mysterious government agency that is trying to hide the paranormal from society.

You know what? It's actually nothing like Romeo and Juliet.

Except no one wants those two together, especially the witches."

AVAILABLE ON AMAZON AND IN KINDLE UNLIMITED!

You made it! Here we are again at the end of this, the second in the series! Thank you so much for reading this far.

Avoiding the topic of coronavirus since we're living that joy (except to say I hope this finds you and yours well), let's talk about Zoom. I have been using it almost exclusively to stay in touch with my peeps, and I have been having fun. First, I torture my publisher by putting up virtual backgrounds of croissants and Krispy Kreme donuts. I can always tell when he catches sight of them because a "Damn you!" comes out of the speakers before I can even see him.

How can I one-up that? Well, in the absence of other income, some farms are renting their llamas, chickens, etc. to crash Zoom meetings. If I wasn't so cheap, we would have visitors at every meeting!

And articles and memes are appearing, reminding people to wear clothes when they Zoom. What the…? How does one forget that? Ah, well.

I didn't mention coffee (much) in my last author notes, but I am addicted. A few days ago, I tried the new Dalgona coffee sensation sweeping the nation. You know the one: water, sugar, coffee creates frothy deliciousness? Put boiling water in your cup and whisk until your wrist falls off? That's the one. I'm here to tell you it's delicious. And even more so with Bailey's and chocolate. Give it a shot! (Although you might leave out the Bailey's if the sun's not over the yardarm, at least somewhere.)

Back to work now. These books don't write themselves. Before I go, I once again want to thank my advance reader team, especially Kelly and Rachel, for their thoughtful suggestions and pointing out story issues. When you write fast to meet the fans' desired timeframe for new releases, teams like this are invaluable. Ultimate reality check. They help make this book (and every book) its best.

I hope you enjoyed Callie's and Ronan's adventure. They will be back. And if you get a moment, drop me a review, please. Those are the lifeblood of any writer. We appreciate you!

Until next time,

Renée

PS: Breaking news: Firefighters rescued a racoon whom they named "Woodrow" from a skate ramp at a Coos Bay, Oregon skate park. This is about as exciting as my world gets, y'all!

The WereWitch Series
Bad Attitude (Book One)
A Bit Aggressive (Book Two)
Too Much Magic (Book Three)

The Callie Hart Series
Thin Ice
Cold Blood

9 781642 029062